CHRISTMAS
IN THE
BOONDOCKS

Book 3 of the Jinx Bay Series

Kay Chandler

A multi-award-winning author

This is a work of fiction. Characters, places, and incidents are products of the author's imagination or use fictitiously.

Scripture taken from the King James Version of the Holy Bible

Cover Design by Chase Chandler

Dedicated to Freta McCall

The characters in the Jinx Bay Series have seen their share of broken promises and shattered dreams. Life doesn't always turn out the way we plan. And who knows that better than my sister-in-law, Freta?

Freta's husband, Ronald (my sweet brother) passed away in his mid-forties. They had a beautiful little girl, Cassy, whom he adored. Then Cassy died. Yet through it all, Freta remains firm in her belief that God is faithful and has a plan for her life. Whenever she's around you'll see a smile and hear a hearty laugh. Not because she's happy. Happiness depends upon circumstances. She smiles because she has the joy of the Lord in her heart. She will tell you Christ is sufficient for all her needs.

As I wrote this novel, I reflected on precious past Christmas's that Freta, and I have shared. Those were joyous times when Camille, Chad, Chase, Matt, Tim, and Cassy were little and my mother, (affectionately known as Mama Lottie) would bake her traditional Jesus' Birthday Cake. It was Red Velvet and as the candles were lit, she'd ask the grandkids:

> "What does the red stand for?"
> They'd reply in unison, "Jesus' blood."
> "What does the white stand for?"
> "Jesus' purity."
> Then, she'd say, "What do the nuts stand for,"
> And they'd laugh and yell, "The McCall's!"

Ronnie played Santa and passed out gifts from under the gaily decorated tree, which Daddy Murray had cut from the farm. Mama Lottie would have dozens of cakes, candies, cookies, and a table fit for a banquet.
Christmas was always their favorite time of year.
One sweet day, we'll all celebrate together again. It'll be a banquet like no other, and the glory of the latter house will be greater than the former house. What a day, glorious day, that will be.

Merry Christmas!
Kay

PROLOGUE

Backstory from BOGGY BAYOU, Book 2
A Story of Redemption

Christmas Eve, 1964, Ronald and Ramona Jones hosted a Christmas dinner for a few close friends and family at Rose Trellis, the lovely Jones' estate in Eufaula, Alabama. Among those attending were their son Deuce; his fiancé Maddie, who was a recent graduate of Troy State College; Peggy Jinright, who lost her husband Frank several months earlier in a fatal automobile accident; Joel Gunter, Ronald's childhood friend; Joel's law partner, Judge Garrison; and the judge's son, Blake.

Joel had gone through bouts of depression, alcoholism, and a gambling addiction. But after becoming acquainted with Blake, a young college drop-out who was estranged from his father, an unlikely bond developed between the two and they wound up saving one another. Judge Garrison, partly out of gratitude for Joel encouraging Blake to turn his life around, and partly because Joel had once been a highly respected attorney, had made Joel an offer he couldn't refuse. He made him a partner in his firm.

Ramona reconciled herself to the fact that her son would not be following the life's path that she'd mapped out for him. Instead, he insisted on operating the Fish Camp on Boggy Bayou in Jinx Bay. Deuce's girlfriend, Maddie, announced she had accepted a temporary position as Assistant Coach at Troy State. Her incarcerated brother's child, Tina, was a resident of the Troy Children's Home.

Deuce's mother had a hunch that Maddie was planning to adopt Tina after she and Deuce married. It wasn't that Ramona didn't like children, and if she felt the child wasn't being properly cared for, she certainly wouldn't want little Tina to remain at the home. But her main concern was for her only son, Deuce. His grandfather had left a legacy with a promise of a good life for his only grandson. Was it fair to burden him down so young with someone else's child? What kind of start in life would that be?

It had been a hard year for several in the room. Not only had Peggy lost her husband, Frank, but her baby boy, Joey, born with Down Syndrome had been snatched away from the hospital and placed in an institution, leaving her with no hope of ever seeing him again. She was still grieving. There were times she felt she should tell Joel the baby was his, but then she'd remember why she couldn't.

But in spite of all the problems of the past year, the day was a joyous one—not because of a table laden with delicious food, or the sounds of Perry Como on the stereo, the gorgeous decorations, or gifts under the tree.

But when Joel arrived, he was holding a bundle. He had accomplished the impossible—he had found the baby and fought the establishment to take him to his mother. Carefully unwrapping the soft blanket, he presented Peggy with her baby. Her heart was full. How could she ever repay him for saving little Joey?

She quickly dismissed the obvious answer, for fear of the consequences.

What would happen if he should ever learn the truth?

CHAPTER 1

October 21, 1965

Deuce Jones, President of the Jinx Bay City Council, rapped his gavel on the podium to quiet the noisy group of attendees. For as long as anyone in the room could remember, there had never been such unrest in the little fishing village on Boggy Bayou. Tempers flared. The subject of discussion was "Christmas Festival or No Christmas Festival." It appeared almost equally divided, with the pros on the right side of the room and the cons on the left. Who would've thought the subject could've conjured up such division?

Granny Noles stood.

Deuce said, "Granny, please sit down and allow Lance to finish. Then, if you have something to say, the floor will recognize you."

"Young man, I'm eighty-eight-years old and my days are numbered. I changed Lance's diapers when he was a baby, and it wasn't all that long ago. He's got plenty of time left and can wait until I have my say. If I don't say it now, I may not live to say it later."

She'd used that same line at every council meeting, church business meeting, or the Jinx Bay Book Club, anytime anyone suggested she wait to be recognized. It never failed to work. Knowing Granny—and they all did—no one would put it past her to hold her breath until she keeled over, just to prove a point.

She reached her hand into the neck of her dress and yanked on what appeared to be a fallen bra strap. "I'm appalled at the way some of you are behaving. However, I understand, probably better than most of you, what's really happening here because I've lived longer than any of you. Ninety-nine percent of us grew up in and around Boggy Bayou. We've gotten along pretty good for the most part, and when we didn't see eye-to-eye on something, we worked it out. Anytime one of us was in trouble, we all came together and met the need. That's the way it ought to be."

Deuce, who was braver than the rest, said, "Granny Noles, the hour is late, and you need to get to your point."

"Just hold your potatoes, young man. If you hadn't interrupted, I'd be there by now. What I'm about to say is long overdue. A lot of ugliness has taken place in this room tonight. Many of you have said things that ought not to be said to a yard dog. But I don't place the blame on any one individual. I blame it on the war."

A couple of men on the left side and a woman on the right side chuckled. At least the two sides were showing a little unity for the first time all night. Granny glanced up from her spectacles. "Don't think I didn't see those of you who snickered, but that don't bother me one iota. You can roll your eyes and hee-haw all you want. But I'm telling you, every time our country goes to war, we see neighbor pitted against neighbor over minor things that wouldn't have amounted to a hill of beans during peacetime. Everyone is on edge. I've witnessed it twice before in my lifetime. And it's happening again, right here in this room."

Granny liked to talk, and no one was willing to shut her up. Perhaps it was because of the fear that she really might die before the next meeting, and the guilt of stopping her would follow them to their graves.

Maybe she was right, or maybe she was wrong, but she told things the way she remembered them. Said she was nineteen, married with a toddler when Mr. Noles went to war in 1918. Shortly after he left, the influenza epidemic killed at least a third of the population of Jinx Bay. She changed it to half the people. According to her, people were on edge—said nasty things they didn't mean—just like today, she added—but in the end, they all came together and helped out where needed.

Granny said in 1939 when WWII broke out, their twenty-three-year old son was drafted, and left home to protect his country. "Food was rationed, which seemed to cause some folks to lose their religion. Hoarding became a problem." She said, "Why, I saw the owner of the Mercantile go take a cow away from a family with babies, because the father owed a dollar or two on a pair of brogans. I declare, rationing brought out the worst in folks. Eventually, they all calmed down and things slowly got back to normal."

There wasn't a person in the room who hadn't heard the story of the cow at least a dozen times, but she loved to tell it, and no one dared to stop her.

Deuce said, "Thank you, Granny, for that stroll down memory lane, but we need to take care of business at hand, or we'll be here until *after* Christmas. Please sit down."

She smiled. "I reckon I said what needed to be said, but if I think of something else, I'll be sure to let you know."

Deuce tried hard not to roll his eyes. "Lance, you still have the floor, if you'd like to continue."

"Thank you, I would."

Just before Granny interrupted, Lance Hightower, who first brought up the idea of a Christmas Festival, laid out suggestions to be considered. It involved encouraging residents to decorate their homes, competing for best inside and outside decorations. He advocated roping off main street—maybe having bands to perform and booths set up for vendors. The longer he spoke, the more animated he became. It was obvious this idea wasn't off the top of his head, but he'd carefully thought through all the details and was eager to spark enthusiasm. "Sure, it'll take a lot of planning and hard work. Maybe y'all think it's too much work for a one day event."

Tom Clark yelled out, "I ain't afraid of work, but this is the stupidest idea you've ever had Lance, and you've had some doozies." A few fellows nodded and mumbled something under their breath, but it didn't deter Lance.

He said, "We could make it last all week, if y'all want. It'll be fun. I promise. All we hear on the news nowadays is negative, and frankly, I feel like we're being waterboarded. I get a horrible feeling sometimes that we're about to cave. I'm ready to have a little fun. Anyone with me?"

Comer said, "Shucks, Lance, I kinda like the idea, but for a whole week? That's crazy."

"That was just a suggestion. A weekend would suit me."

Jennie Lou said, "What do you do at a Christmas Festival? I've never been to one."

Lance said, "There are dozens of things we can do. We could hold a Bazaar where people can come and buy homemade Christmas gifts. Miss Annie makes some of the prettiest crocheted doilies that I've ever seen. My wife has bought several from her. They'd be a hit. And Comer's bird houses are unlike any you could buy in a store, and have you seen the doll houses he makes? Oh, and did I mention Granny Noles bakes the best cakes I've ever eaten? Well, you get the idea."

Frazier raised his hand. "I think it's a great idea. My Jennie Lou brings home a five-gallon bucket of Georgia Clay, every time we visit her folks. She's quite the artist and her clay pots and bowls are as pretty as any you'll find anywhere. I bought her a small kiln for her birthday, and it's a real experience just to watch her take that lump of clay and turn it into something beautiful. Her earthenware would make excellent gifts."

Deuce said, "Thank you, Frazier. Any questions?"

Comer stood. "Not a question. I'd just like to say I like the idea. We have a lot of talent in this little community. We could hold a talent show, and maybe all gather to sing Christas Carols at the lighting of a Christmas Tree on the square. "

Granny Noles said, "I thank you for mentioning my cakes, Lance. Nothing delights me more than to see folks enjoying something I've baked. And If I could sell a few home baked goods, then that would help me buy those grand-chilun a little something to go under the tree. Those are all excellent suggestions you men have made, but the one thing I'd love to see would be a live Nativity Scene. You know. . . let the young'uns dress up like characters in the Christmas Story." Several breathed sighs of relief when it appeared she'd said all she wanted to say.

Lance said, "Great idea, Granny."

Tom Clark, owner of the hardware stormed up to the front and faced the crowd. "What in Heaven's name is wrong with you people? You want to party like everything is hunky-dory? Have you forgotten we're at war? Our boys are off fighting for their lives against a country which employs guerilla tactics and uses the dense jungle as a cover—a terrain which is unfamiliar to our soldiers." His voice quivered. "Our sons are being shot down like those little metal ducks at the Fair that keep rolling by while you stand there pulling the trigger, hoping to win a Teddy Bear. The Viet Cong are going for the prize, and our boys are sitting ducks."

The woman behind him reached over and patted him on the back.

Terry said, "I agree with you Tom. I don't know about the rest of you, but it makes me sick on my stomach to even think about our young men trying to maneuver a dense jungle halfway around the world, while trying to fight off an enemy that employs the use of chemical weapons. It's insane. You can count me out. I'll be at home on my knees—not at some festival, whooping it up."

Heads on the left side of the room nodded in agreement, and people were saying things like, "Well said, Terry. Me, too. Thank you, Terry. Amen, Brother."

CHAPTER 2

The feedback coming from Tom's peers on the left-side of the room seemed to give him his second wind. He shook his finger toward the folks on the right side of the room. "I must say, I'm surprised at the callousness of many of you here, tonight. It's a cold-hearted, selfish individual who would even consider such a crazy notion of partying, as if all is well in the world. I would've thought the lives of our young men would mean more to all of you than that."

Tempers were getting out of control and the chatter on the left side of the room was already out of hand. Deuce rapped his gavel. "Hey, let's not have any name-calling. I think everyone has had ample time to say what you came here to say. Are we ready to take a vote?"

Tom shouted, "You can shut us up, Deuce, but you can't stop us from feeling the way we do. How can anyone in America even consider celebrating when our boys are being killed in a war that's none of our business?" Tom's wife, who appeared unable to hold back her tears, rushed out of the room sobbing.

Tom and Lila had lost their only son in Normandy over twenty years ago, leaving a wife and young son. Then last Monday, they received word that their beloved twenty-one-year-old grandson, Tommy, was one of the three-hundred Americans killed in the Battle of la Drang Valley. Citizens on the left side of the room nodded in solidarity, while the citizens on the right side quietly bowed their heads, many with tears in their eyes.

Mildred Smith, owner of a local eatery and seated on the right side, raised her hand, and was recognized. "Mr. President, let me begin by assuring Tom that there's not a single person in this room who isn't mourning with him and Lila over young Tommy's death. We all loved Tommy. We watched him grow up into a fine, caring, and loving young man."

Tom blurted, "Mildred, how can you say you loved my grandson, yet you sit there with that bunch who wants to celebrate and party as if his death and the death of hundreds more like him means nothing?"

Mildred's bottom lip quivered. "I'm sorry, I can't do this—" She sat down. A woman sitting next to her reached over and patted Mildred on the shoulder and whispered, "He's hurting but not because of anything you said. You did fine."

Deuce said, "If I may, I'd like to speak for Mildred, since I believe I understand where she's coming from. Mildred isn't the only one in this room who has wept bitterly over the news of

Tommy's death. Although there were hundreds of other American sons to die, Tommy was one of us. I lived in Jinx Bay when I was sixteen and he was fifteen. We played baseball together in the field back of the Feed Store. He was an outstanding athlete, but that's not the main thing I remember about him. It was his kindness and how people seemed to flock to him. He was generous to a fault. I saw him take off a new pair of tennis shoes and tell a kid to try them on. The Bible says if you have two coats, and someone has none, then give him a coat. It says nothing about if you only have one pair of shoes, but Tommy walked home that day, barefoot. I moved back to Eufaula shortly afterward, and lost contact with both boys, but it's something I'll never forget."

A woman on the back row on the left side jumped up. "Mr. President, may I speak?"

Deuce said, "The floor recognizes Mrs. Daisy Wimples."

"Sir, I came here ready to vote against decorating the town for Christmas. I don't feel like celebrating, because I have a son fighting in Vietnam also, and I live in fear from day to day that I'll get the same news that the Clarks received. But I want Mr. Clark to know that the day his grandson went home without shoes was the same day my son came home wearing shoes.

My husband had left us six months earlier, and I moved here with my fifteen-year-old boy. It was about this time of year, and he'd outgrown his shoes. He enrolled in school and came home from that first day, asking for money to buy a pair, but I could either feed him or put shoes on his feet. I chose to feed him. My heart broke every morning as I watched him out the window walking to school. I knew he was embarrassed, although he never said another word to me about it. I began to pray for God to provide shoes for my sweet boy.

But he met some really nice kids here in Jinx Bay, who invited him to play ball after school. One day, he came home wearing a brand new pair of sneakers. I asked where he got them and he said, 'Mama, all I can tell you is that I didn't steal them. I promise."

"I knew my boy and I knew he'd walk over hot coals barefooted before he would steal someone else's shoes.

He said, 'The person who gave them to me made me promise I wouldn't tell anyone where they came from.' Then my boy said, 'Mama, he trusted me not to tell, and now I want you to trust me.' She looked down and twisted a handkerchief in her hands. "Well, I had no choice, since I had trusted God to give my boy shoes and until this day, I haven't known how God got those shoes to my Kevin."

Deuce smiled. "Yes ma'am. His name was Kevin. Are we ready to vote?"

Kevin's mother said, "Just one more thing. I came here to vote against a celebration, but knowing my Kevin, and in loving memory of Mr. Tom and Mrs. Lila's grandson, I'd say if our boys could vote today, they'd vote in favor of celebrating Christ's birth, not cancelling Christmas." She excused herself as she avoided stepping on feet while making her way from the center of the row toward the aisle. "I believe there's room for me on the other side."

One by one, others joined her on the right. Some were laughing, some were crying, but it was all the hugging that made it evident the town was once again, uniting.

Daisy Wimples said, "We talked as if it might be downtown, but I'd like to suggest another place. Why not have it at the Fish Camp, and set up booths along the Bayou? There are already lights out there."

When Granny stood, sighs could be heard. She said, "That's a great idea. There's a Gazebo near the docks where the young'uns can hold their little pageant. We can call it Christmas in the Boondocks."

She got a standing ovation.

Deuce called for a vote and all but two people—who quietly slipped out the door—voted in favor of the motion.

CHAPTER 3

Deuce sat in his office, going over the books, and wondering why he'd waited so long to fire the incompetent bookkeeper. Betsy was great at baking cakes and cookies, but unless the auditors had a sweet tooth, they were not going to be impressed.

There were pages after pages in the ledger filled with incorrect information. Some vendors' names were listed without any indication of what they had purchased. There was no accounting of the order, and nothing listed under the received column. Just a company name. That was enough to worry him. How much did they order? How much did they pay? There was absolutely no way to tell.

But then he discovered something really frightening that apparently had been taking place for quite a while. The woman couldn't multiply, even with the help of an adding machine. Where she came up with some of the figures in the ledger was a mystery.

One example was Fresh Fish, Inc. They ordered seventy pounds of flounder for their trucker to pick up. He was given a signed check to be filled in by the seller. Flounder sells for $.15 a pound. Betsy made out the signed check for the amount of $32.15 and the driver, who no doubt didn't get past third grade, had no idea it was wrong. And that wasn't the only vendor who was charged an exorbitant amount. The sad fact was that it hadn't just begun. Some of the glaring errors went back to before Boyd died.

Deuce knew it would be just a matter of time before these companies would check their books and feel that he'd been taking advantage of them. He'd heard of people going to jail for much less. He had known all along that Betsy wasn't much of a secretary, but he never dreamed anyone so incompetent would have applied for a bookkeeping position. Before Boyd died, he admitted Betsy was incapable of fulfilling her duties, but he continued to clean up after her.

Then when Deuce took over, he expected everyone to continue doing their job, while he worked on becoming proficient with the duties of an operational manager.

He hardly had time to do learn all that was expected of him, and now it was going to take more time than he could spare to straighten out the mess Betsy had created. The first thing he needed to do was to issue checks to all the vendors who had been overcharged before they realized what had been going on and reported him to the authorities. It would be a time-consuming task, but no way could he leave that job to Betsy. She'd done enough harm. He had to let her go and find a quick replacement.

Sweat gathered on his forehead and dripped from the tip of his nose. Feeling hot around the collar, he unbuttoned the first couple of buttons on his shirt and wiped the back of his neck with a handkerchief.

Then slamming the books shut, he vaulted from his chair to open all the windows. The air-conditioner had been on all day, yet the thermostat had not moved from 79 degrees. Deuce had put off having the air-conditioner worked on. It was October, for crying out loud. Even Northwest Florida should be cooling off somewhat by now. So why was the temperature today hovering in August digits?

Strange, the humidity never bothered him when he lived in Jinx Bay as a teenager. But after joining the Navy and coming back, he could hardly breathe. So why did he stay? In spite of the annoying heat, he admitted to himself there was no place on earth where he'd rather be. However, for the past hour, he'd questioned his sanity. Today had been hectic, for sure, but it wouldn't always be this way. Or would it? Boyd told him Betsy wasn't capable of doing the job. He should've fired her.

He walked back over to his desk, sat down, and reached for the phone. But before dialing the number, he slammed the receiver back on the cradle. He'd never thought of himself as a procrastinator until now. He had a job to do, and there was no need in wasting any more time.

It had been easy to blame Boyd for not firing Betsy, but hadn't he had more than enough reason to let the girl go? Yet the thought of firing someone, even someone as incapable of doing their job as Betsy, made his stomach tie in knots. But it had to be done. Determined not to put it off any longer, he would march over to the storage room, which had been converted into the bookkeeper's office, and chit-chat for a couple of minutes about the weather before getting down to the nitty-gritty.

Deuce had carefully rehearsed his little speech, hoping that it wouldn't sound too harsh. After all, he was sure she hadn't purposely cheated the customers with the intent of sending him to prison for life. She just didn't have what it took to keep books. Wasn't that as much his fault as it was hers? He should've been paying closer attention to details.

He'd be as gentle as possible and pray that she wouldn't start crying. He hated to see a woman cry. Perhaps he should offer her a bonus. That sounded good. A goodbye bonus. Maybe twenty-five dollars? It would be worth it to see her walk out the door.

Before he reached the storage room, he could hear raucous laughter coming from inside. Deuce walked in and found four of his deck hands holding paper plates laden with baked goodies. Four platters of delicious-looking sweets sat on top of the filing cabinet. Crumbs were strewn all over the floor. He yelled, "What's going on in here?" Then throwing up his hands, he said, "Don't answer that. I can see what's going on."

Betsy appeared oblivious to anything unusual. She said, "Hi, bossman. Come fix you a plate." Then giggling she said, "If you don't hurry, there won't be anything left."

Anger swelled within him. He forgot his speech and blurted, "You may find those words to be prophetic, Betsy. There's probably *not* going to be anything, or anyone left in here after today. You four guys are fired. All four of you, and as for you Betsy, please clean out your desk. You can go with them. I've put up with this longer than I ever should have, and it's not as if I haven't given all of you fair warning."

The fellows all began to give excuses, but Deuce had heard all he wanted to hear. He turned and stormed back to his office. He plopped down in the big swivel chair and thought about the first day he sat there. It was a week before Boyd died. Deuce recalled rubbing his hand across the beautiful mahogany desk and dreaming of one day being able to see his name on the door. His dream was fast becoming a nightmare.

In the past few weeks, he had discovered that managing the day-to-day operations of a large fishing industry was no easy task. He had insisted to his dad that he was capable of running the camp. But was he? What would his father think now, when he discovered he was four hands short and had fired the bookkeeper. Well, he didn't have to find out. Did he?

Deuce hurried outside, jumped in his pickup, and drove over to Cannery Road, knowing the deckhands all lived in the cottages and would be clearing out their belongings. He pulled up to Cottage #4 first and knocked on the door. A guy they all called Bozer opened the door, and said, "I wondered how long it would take you to get here, bossman."

Deuce had never minded being called bossman by the deckhands, but today it sounded more like a smirk. "Okay, so I acted impulsively. I apologize. I need you, Bozer."

"I know. But we owe you an apology as well. We've been taking advantage of you and that was wrong. I can't speak for the other fellows, but I'll make you a promise, I won't be goofing off in Betsy's office anymore."

"Thanks. But Betsy will be gone."

"But bossman, it ain't all her fault. I reckon she wouldn't have out done herself if we hadn't encouraged her."

"I'm not letting her go simply because she insisted on turning the office into a bakery. She's being terminated because she's not a bookkeeper. But I reckon I'd better stop gabbing and go tell the other fellows not to pack up and leave. I need them."

Bozer laughed. "Oh, they ain't packing up. They know you need 'em. They're just waiting for you to find out. You can get on back. I'll go tell 'em it's time to go."

CHAPTER 4

Candy McCoy sat with her boss, Jack Ainsley, in a backroom at an out-of-the-way dive somewhere between Montgomery and Birmingham, Alabama. She rubbed her eyes.

Jack said, "I'm sorry, Candy. Honest, I am. Please don't cry."

"I'm not crying, Jack. All this cigarette smoke is burning my eyes. Can we please go somewhere else?"

"Honey, you know I can't risk being seen. My face is all over billboards. I'm not difficult to recognize. Had you rather go outside and sit in the car?"

"Yes, thank you."

Candy had a good thing going, but she had a feeling it was fast coming to an end. While a student at Massey Draughn School of Business in Montgomery, Alabama, the school office had sent her on an interview with Jack Ainsley, the CEO of Alabama's fastest growing bank.

She was hired immediately and began working parttime as a teller, while attending classes. Three months later, when she was told Mr. Ainsley wanted to see her in his office, she worried that her performance had not been to his satisfaction. To the contrary. She discovered not only did he praise her for her wonderful job, he gave her a promotion, with a raise.

Candy had grown up in a home that some might call 'broken,' but she had often insisted that something that never existed couldn't possibly break. She claimed to have never had a home. If she had a father, her mother didn't seem to know who he was, and as for her mother, she insisted that Candy call her by her first name, not wanting her constant flow of "boyfriends," to know she was old enough to have a grown daughter. Candy didn't know exactly what it would take to make a home, but she did know she had nothing to build upon.

When she was in the fifth grade, her teacher told them if they studied hard and made good grades, they could become anything they wanted to be. That was the day Candy decided she wanted to be rich. She was tired of going home to a dirty, cold shanty, and having to turn on the oven before school to get a little heat in the house, while her mother slept off another drunk.

She was tired of kids making fun of her for wearing the same dress every day and for having the soles of her shoes duct taped on to keep them from flopping when she walked. Well, if making good grades was the only thing standing in the way of her having pretty clothes and living in a beautiful house, then by George, she'd make good grades. And she did. That same fifth grade schoolteacher, who was aware of her circumstances, had kept her eye on Candy and upon graduation, paid for her to attend the Montgomery business school. She was at the top of her class at the end of every reporting period.

After she finished school, Mr. Ainsley told her if she'd agree to stay and work at the bank, he'd move her into her own office, with an even more prestigious position. It was a new position, with a new title, and less work. Candy was beginning to understand her teacher had known what she was talking about.

Mr. Ainsley praised her for her outstanding performance and began to spend almost as much time in her office as he did his own. He took her into his confidence. His wife Anna had left him, and he was devastated to the point of tears at times. Candy knew what it felt like to have someone disappoint you, and although she felt inept at knowing how to comfort him, he told her she always knew the right words to say to make him feel better. He insisted she refer to him as Jack when they were alone, and he'd always give her big hugs and thank her for being the best friend he'd ever had.

Candy couldn't say exactly when the friendship turned into something more, but one thing led to another. He moved her into a penthouse in Montgomery. Next came the Thunderbird. The raise. The credit cards. But always in between the gifts, was the promise of marriage. A promise which never came to fruition.

Candy had seen the looks when she walked through the bank.

Then came the accusations. Shopping in a department store one day, she heard a woman whisper to her friend. "That's her. That's Jack's bimbo." Her heart broke. She and Jack apparently hadn't been as discreet as they thought.

When she finally faced the truth she realized the only difference between her and her mother was that she found a rich sugar daddy, while her mother picked up her benefactors standing in the welfare lines. She tossed and turned all night, conflicted.

As soon as she got back to the penthouse after work the next day, she called Jack. "We need to talk."

He came over immediately.

"Jack, I can't do this anymore."

"Do what? What are you talking about?"

"I think you know. I thought having money would make me happy. Well, you've provided me with more money than I ever dreamed possible. But you know what? I'm not happy."

"I'm sorry, baby. What can I do?"

"You can let me go." She reached in her purse and pulled out the keys. "Here's the keys to the car."

He sat on the white velvet sofa with his face buried in his hands. "I'm sorry, Candy. I'll miss you."

That was it? That was all he had to say? She had expected she'd have to convince him it was for the best. Did he not even care that she was leaving? Did he have him another bimbo in the wings? This hadn't gone down right. She was expecting to have to console him; yet he needed no consoling. Suddenly, she felt very stupid for believing the lies.

Then, the truth came out. He was getting ready to break it off with her. He simply hadn't found the right time to tell her. He said he and his ex-wife were getting back together. He told her that Anna knew all about their relationship and he had promised her that he'd help find Candy another job in another town. "I'm sorry."

"Don't be." Candy swallowed hard. Although this was not what she had expected to hear, the thing that surprised her most was that she wasn't sorry that he and his wife were getting back together. Perhaps she should be angry, but instead, she was happy for him. Truly. She didn't hate Jack. Why should she? Though she found it hard to admit, even to herself, she couldn't deny the truth. She had known what she was doing was wrong, but denying the truth had made it easier to live with herself.

He handed the keys back to her. "You keep the car. You earned it."

The words stung. But he was right. She had earned it. She paid for it with her good name.

He laid five-hundred dollars on the coffee table and said, "I want to give you this, but I'll need the credit cards. I've cleared it with Anna, and she suggested we give you the car, because as she said, it's your way out of town. But she insisted that I get the credit cards back."

She handed him the cards and pointed to the hundred dollar bills. "Pick up your money, Jack. I'll get by."

"It's a gift, Candy. Please take it." He left and she began

30

packing her things. She stuck five-hundred, seventy-five dollars and twenty-three cents in her purse with no thought of where she'd go.

She rode as far south as she could go in Alabama, then crossed the Florida line and decided to keep driving until she came to a place that felt right. But would anything ever feel right again? It was late in the evening as she drove across a bridge and saw the sun going down over the Gulf of Mexico. A peace that she hadn't thought possible came over her. It was as if someone was whispering in her ear, "This is it."

She saw a sign, "Welcome to Walton Beach, God's Country."

God's Country? Yes! That's exactly what it felt like. Home at last.

She saw a 'For Rent sign on a boarding house, stopped and secured a room. The next day, she'd begin a search for a place to work. The only thing she'd rule out would be the banks. She'd had access to money. This time, she'd seek access to peace. In her mind, she imagined working in a quiet, peaceful environment, perhaps close to the water, since that's what she saw when the stress and shame of the past two years left her, and a renewed sense of hope filled the deep dark hole.

CHAPTER 5

Deuce didn't know whether to be angry at their smugness or laugh because his men knew him better than he knew himself. He didn't have time to dwell on the issue. He had to find a bookkeeper and find one quick.

He drove over to the Okaloosa County Employment Agency. The fellow he spoke with assured him he had someone in mind that he thought Deuce would be pleased with.

Deuce said, "She can't cook, can she?"

The man looked confused. "I thought you were looking for a bookkeeper, not a housekeeper."

"Forget it. It's a private joke. You wouldn't get it. But you're right, I want a bookkeeper. I want her to know how to use an adding machine. And knowing the difference in debits and credits would also be a big plus."

The fellow laughed. "I'm guessing your last girl must've had other talents."

"You're right. She could be the Sous Chef for Julia Childs. Maybe even take over her TV show. But she's definitely not a bookkeeper."

"The woman I have in mind has just recently located here. I don't know if she'll be interested in driving to Jinx Bay, but it wouldn't be more than seven or eight miles, since she's staying in a rooming house, halfway between here and there."

Deuce's brow crinkled. "She does have a high school degree, I hope."

Flashing a wink, he said, "Whew! You have some tough stipulations. Number one, you won't allow her to cook at work, and she has to be able to cipher. Now, you're insisting she can't be a dropout. That's a lot to ask."

Deuce didn't find his joke entertaining. "I want to make sure I know what I'm getting! Obviously, my predecessor failed to ask the right questions when he hired our present bookkeeper."

"Sorry. I shouldn't have made light of your dilemma. I'm sure it hasn't been very funny. But as for Miss McCoy, she not only has a high school degree, she's a graduate of Massey Draughn Business School in Montgomery. Her report card was included with her resume, and she was an honor roll student. She also worked parttime for a big bank in Montgomery while in school, and if I remember correctly, she said she stayed with them a year or two afterward and moved up quickly, earning several merit raises."

"Sounds like she had a good thing going. Would you happen to know why she would've left Montgomery to come to the Boondocks?"

"I don't make a habit of dabbling in my client's private affairs, and I believe that would be dabbling."

"Well, if it takes dabbling for me to find a woman who can work fulltime and is capable of straightening out the mess the former so-called bookkeeper left us, then I might have to become a dabbler. My books are in serious trouble, and I need competent help ASAP."

"Trust me, sir, if you'll give her a chance, I think you'll see she's exactly what you need. I'll admit I was stunned by her qualifications. She's the most impressive client I've had pass through here in quite a while."

"Sounds good. Would you mind giving her a call and seeing if we can set up an interview?"

"I'll do it now." After making the call, he hung up, reared back in his chair, and said, "You'd better get on back to the Fish Camp and get her room ready. She said to give her ten minutes and she'd meet you at your office."

Looking him squarely in the eye, Deuce said, "You seem pretty sure that I'll hire her and that she'll take the job."

"I'd bet on it."

Deuce stood, shook his hand, and headed back to Jinx Bay, thinking that was a most peculiar conversation.

Deuce left the employment agency with the worst case of heartburn he'd ever had. He stopped by the grocery store to pick up a package of anti-acid tablets before driving back to the Fish Camp.

He pulled up in front of his office and saw a gorgeous 1957 red Thunderbird convertible parked out front. He got out and walked around, admiring every little detail. It was his dream car. Had been since it first came out when he was in high school. *"One day, baby,"* he mumbled to himself.

He assumed it belonged to some big-wig restaurant owner, who had shown up to either order a mess of fish or complain about his bill.

He hoped he could get rid of him quickly before the girl arrived for the interview. If she was everything the guy at the Employment Office said she was, he didn't want her first impression to be of her prospective boss arguing with a client.

Walking inside, he was met by a beautiful young woman, dressed as if she'd just stepped out of a magazine. "Hello, I'm Deuce Jones. May I help you, ma'am?"

"I hope so. I'm Candy McCoy. The Employment Agency sent me over here to speak to someone about a job as a bookkeeper. Would that be you?"

He attempted to hide his surprise. "Uh, yes ma'am. I was expecting you." He looked out the window. "Is that T-bird yours?"

"Yes sir."

"Please, cut out the sir."

"I will when you cut out the ma'am."

"Gotcha." Feeling embarrassed, he walked around and pulled out a chair. "Please have a seat."

He walked around and sat at his desk. "I need a bookkeeper. Could you tell me about your experience?"

"I worked parttime at a bank in Montgomery while attending Business School in pursuit of an Executive Secretarial Degree. I graduated with straight A's in bookkeeping. Math has always been my best subject, so working with numbers has come easy for me. I'm a speed typer and am proficient in Gregg Shorthand."

"You sound perfect. In fact, with those qualifications, I'm not sure we could pay you what you're worth."

She giggled. "I'm quite sure you can't. I'm afraid if I try to find a job that can pay me what I'm worth, I'll be unemployed the rest of my life. And frankly, I'd like to stay busy while walking around on this earth."

Deuce didn't know whether to laugh with her or to wish her well and watch her walk out the door. The girl either had a peculiar sense of humor, or she was very confident in her abilities. He hoped for the latter.

He was almost embarrassed to tell her what the job paid, because it certainly wouldn't be enough to make payments on that shiny sports car of hers. To his surprise, she didn't bat an eye before saying, "What time shall I report for work?"

He let out a heavy breath. Could this girl be real? He said, "Why don't I show you around the Fish Camp and introduce you to the ladies working in the Cannery, and the fellows cleaning up the boats. The fishermen are still out, but you'll eventually have an opportunity to meet them all. We have a great group of employees. Do you have any questions?"

"Yes. I do have a couple. The first one is, 'Where is my office?'"

"Oh, that. Uh . . . well, I'll have you a desk in my office before tomorrow. The previous bookkeeper was way back in the storage room, but I discovered that was very inconvenient. Besides, I need the storage room for . . . storage."

"Would you like for me to help move the desk?"

"No, I'll have a couple of the guys do it. You said you had a few questions."

"Yes. I've always loved coming to Florida with my daddy, so when I finished school, I decided there's no other place I'd rather live than near Walton Beach."

"So, you plan to live there?"

"No, Jinx Bay is close enough. I could be happy here. By the way, I saw a sign on Cannery Road as I was riding in, so I drove down and there's a cute little cottage for rent. Would you happen to know the person I should talk to about renting it?"

"It's very small."

"Yes. It would be perfect."

Why was he trying to talk her out of it? Yet who could imagine a tenant of the Fish Camp Cottages having a Thunderbird parked in front? Most of the tenants didn't even own cars.

"Then it's yours."

"So, who do I contact?"

"Jones' Industries owns them, and we rent them out to employees. If you like, we'll include it in your package."

"Thank you. I'd like that."

"Then it's settled."

"Just one more thing. Can you direct me to a good place to eat? I'm starving."

Deuce walked her outside and pointed toward the right. "If you go past Cannery Road, then take the first left and— "Why don't you follow me? I haven't eaten either. There's a popular little diner called Mildred's. We all eat there. I think you'll like it."

"Great. Thanks, Mr. Jones."

"Call me Deuce." He smiled, anticipating the next question. "Just don't ask where my name came from."

"I won't. I'll assume you're the second in your family to be named whatever it is you're named."

He walked over and opened her car door for her. He hoped he wasn't drooling. "Nice wheels."

"It was a graduation present from my daddy."

Deuce got in his truck and kept one eye on the road, and one on the red convertible following him. What was a girl like her, doing in a place like this, instead of a fancy office in a city like Montgomery or Tallahassee? She hadn't taken the job for the money, that was for sure. Besides, with parents who could afford to gift her with a T-Bird convertible, it was quite conceivable that she didn't have to work at all. Why should he question her motives? Maybe she liked the idea of working around the water. No one could understand that better than he.

He knew the fellows were gonna rag him about hiring such a beauty and would never believe her looks had nothing to do with her getting the job. With her credentials, he would've hired an ugly old hag. He wasn't interested in what she looked like. All he cared about was that she'd taken courses in bookkeeping, typing, and filing, and was at the top of her class. He chuckled. "They won't believe a word of it, but it's true." He scratched his head. "It *is* true."

CHAPTER 6

Candy kept her eye on the truck in front of her and decided there must be something to this prayer thingy after all. When she drove out of Montgomery and cried out to God for help, she had no reason to expect him to hear her. After all, she was no Annie Armstrong or Lottie Moon. Funny, how those two names stuck in her mind. They were names of missionaries she recalled hearing about as a child, when the church bus came around to pick her up.

If landing in Jinx Bay wasn't a direct answer from heaven, she couldn't imagine what else it could be.

She recalled doing a lot of praying late at night when she was a little girl. She prayed for all sorts of things like shoes and hair bows and hot meals, but mainly she prayed for her mama to love her. Eventually she stopped expecting God to hear her. Why would he?

But maybe it was time to start believing again, seeing how things had worked out for her good. She couldn't have searched the world over and found a better place to escape from her past than to hide out at a Fish Camp in the boondocks. And the supervisor, or whatever hat he wore, seemed like a nice fellow. A little naïve, maybe, but nice.

Town consisted of one street, and there was no Gayfer's, no Davison's, no Macy's, no Rich's—not even a Woolworth's, but what difference did it make? It wasn't as if she needed clothes, and besides, who would she be trying to impress? No one, that's who.

All she was interested in was to have a place in which she could retreat, and what better place than in a sleepy little town where no one cared who you were, what you wore, or more importantly, what you might be running away from.

Candy parked her car beside Deuce's at the restaurant, but he was already out and ready to open the door for her. He stuck his hand inside and rubbed the soft leather seat. "Wow, what a beauty."

Candy smiled. "Why, thank you, sir."

Deuce bit his lip. "Uh . . ."

She giggled. "Oh! You were referring to the car, weren't you?"

He wasn't easily embarrassed, but this was embarrassing. "Actually, I was, but I could've easily been referring to the owner." He was glad she dropped the topic before he put his foot in his mouth once again. Why he found her intimidating, he couldn't say. There was just something about her that made him get all tongue-tied. Every time he looked at her, he felt like a kid sneaking a look at something he had no business seeing. She was just that lovely. Not that there was anything evil about her. In fact, she looked almost angelic, or at least the way he perceived angels to look. Those without wings, of course.

When they walked inside Mildred's every head in the diner turned.

Deuce led her over to the table he normally occupied near the plate glass window. She whispered, "Why is everyone looking? Do I have something on my face?"

Their eyes met, then embarrassed, he shifted his gaze. "It's a small town. They're wondering what the beautiful woman driving a T-Bird is doing in Jinx Bay."

"Well, you're sweet, but I'm sure that's not what's on their mind."

"Then what would you guess?"

"I think they all know you and are wondering if there's a new love in your life."

Deuce smirked. "They know better."

"Why would you say that?"

"Because they all know I'm engaged to be married."

"I think I've embarrassed you. Again."

"Don't be silly. I'm not embarrassed."

She said, "Then Congratulations."

"For what? Not being embarrassed?"

"No, silly. Your impending marriage."

"Oh. That. Thanks."

42

"When is the big day?"

"We've planned it for this Spring." He picked up the menu. "I think they've all stopped staring. So, what would you like?"

"What do you suggest?"

"I plan on getting a hamburger and fries, but the daily special is always good if you're hungry for a meat and three."

"I'll take the hamburger."

In a few minutes, Deuce and Candy were sharing funny stories about their childhood, and although he discovered they had very little in common, he loved her sense of humor. She was easy to talk to. He told her all about the town's plans for a Christmas Festival, and she seemed giddy with excitement.

She said, "I want to help. Could you connect me with someone on one of the committees? I love Christmas."

He decided he'd done a very good thing. He had not only found a top-notch bookkeeper, but she was a great conversationalist. She'd be able to talk to their clients and would be a real asset to the company. He didn't always use the most tactful responses when dealing with belligerent salespeople. She'd be perfect for helping settle disputes.

He just hoped he could keep her. She was worth more than what Betsy was paid, that was for sure. "When would you like to move into the cottage on Cannery Road?"

"I'm fine staying at the rooming house, but if it's available now, then tomorrow after work, I could bring my things over. I saw that it was furnished, but if the job works out and you decide to keep me, would you have a place to store the present furniture, in order that I can furnish it with my own?"

"No problem at all. Just let me know when you're ready and I'll have some of the fellows go over and load up what's in there and put it in the storage room. When you decide to leave, we can put the old furniture back in."

She grinned. "Who said I would decide to leave?"

"Well, I'd like to think you'd settle in and make it home, but I'm trying to be realistic. Most of the folks who rent those cottages come here with nothing more than the clothes on their backs. I moved into one when I first took this job, but a while back I moved into a cabin in the woods that belongs to my father."

"Cabin in the woods. I like the sound of it. I'm sure it's nice."

Deuce chuckled. "Then I presented it wrong. It suits me, but I wouldn't refer to it as nice. However, it holds some special memories. It's where my girlfriend and I first became acquainted."

"I love a good love story. I'd like to hear it."

He laughed. "You wouldn't understand."

"Try me."

"Okay, here goes. My dad met her at Mildred's when she walked over to his table. He thought she was a prostitute."

"Really?" Her brow crinkled. "Are we still talking about the girl you plan to marry."

"Yep. Told you that you wouldn't understand."

"I'm capable of understanding more than you might know. This is interesting. Please continue."

44

"Well, she let him know quickly that she was desperate but not that desperate. She left in a huff, and after he'd eaten, he started to drive over to my Cottage and saw her walking in the rain. He stopped and after arguing with her to get in, she did."

"Are you saying he decided he was right about her?"

"No. He realized he was wrong. She had approached him because she was running from an abusive man, she had no money, and she was hungry. She had hoped he'd buy her a sandwich."

Then noticing Candy's dubious expression, Deuce added, "No strings attached."

"I gather he took her back to the restaurant?"

"He would have, but the restaurant was closed. So, he took her to my cottage and asked me to gather up some bacon and eggs and he was going to take her to the Cabin in the woods, cook her something to eat, and let her stay overnight."

She rolled her eyes. "With him, naturally."

He laughed. "You keep trying to find something sinister going on. This is my father, we're talking about. He's not the cheating kind."

Candy mumbled, "Every man is the cheating kind when he thinks he can do it without getting caught."

"Not true. You have a very low opinion of men, don't you?"

"No, I was teasing. I'm sure your dad had nothing but good intentions."

"True. He has a big heart and when he learned she was hungry, the only thing in his mind was to get her something to eat..

I got a few groceries out of the fridge and rode over to the Cabin with them. And before you ask, No, I had nothing on my mind except to ride with Dad, which I felt would make him more comfortable than being alone with a strange woman at the cabin. He's very keen on avoiding all appearances of evil."

"Well, aren't you sweet to want to save him from vicious gossip?"

"Did I hear a bit of sarcasm in your voice?"

"I'm sorry, Deuce. You'll have to forgive me. I suppose I do sometimes tend to see the worst in folks. But I believe you. Truly, I do."

"Well, don't apologize too soon. I may have to explain my actions before this conversation is finished."

"Sounds intriguing. I can hardly wait."

"I volunteered to cook, and Maddie—that's her name—Maddie Anderson—insisted on helping me. We hit it off immediately. She has a great sense of humor, and I've never had as much fun cooking breakfast foods, or ever done such a lousy job of it. We burned everything, but we were having fun doing it. It was the beginning of a lasting friendship.

She went to work for Mildred until she earned enough money to go back home to Troy, where she was in her senior year at Troy State College. One thing led to another, and I gave her a ring for Christmas the night of her December graduation.

I'm sorry. I didn't mean to go into such depth about my love life. I'm sure that was more information than you needed or wanted."

"To the contrary. I love to hear you talk, and I'm the one who asked for your love story. I can understand even better now, why the Cabin in the woods would mean so much to you. I'd love to see it sometime."

"Sure, but don't expect much. It's nothing to write home about." He looked outside the window. "It looks like it might be fixing to rain. Would you like for me to run out and put the top up on your car?"

"Thanks. That's a good idea. I'm through eating and am ready to go if you are."

CHAPTER 7

Maddie Anderson sat near the window in her Troy apartment, watching the rain, while holding what she perceived to be the most important letter of her lifetime.

She had put off responding for as long as she possibly could, since her answer could alter the direction of her life. Not could but would. She'd read the letter with an Auburn University letterhead countless times since receiving it a week earlier. As much as she wanted to respond with a resounding yes, yes, yes, she understood too well that once she replied in the affirmative, she could forget about the happily-ever-after with Deuce Jones. Is that really what she wanted to do?

She'd changed her mind a dozen times, but after today, whichever decision she made would be final. There'd be no turning back. If only her friend Josie were here to tell her what she should do. Josie had not only been her roommate at Troy, but she was more like a sister. Maddie could tell her anything, and she always felt more confident after their talks. How she missed her.

Maddie was an Assistant Coach of the women's' basketball team at Troy State College, her alma mater. Her girls were winning games, yet there were times when she felt like giving up. Was this one of those times?

She enjoyed working with the girls, and loved coaching, but the sport wasn't gaining the popularity as quickly as she had hoped. There were afternoons when the seats in the gym were completely empty, and even if a couple of students happened to show up, they seemed more interested in visiting with one another than paying attention to what was taking place on the court.

As much as Maddie wanted to see things change, not many sports fans regarded women's basketball as a legitimate collegiate sport. Many college teams still played half-court, which she found to be extremely frustrating. Although some schools had gone to full court, it was slow to catch on. Maddie had hopes that in time the sport would become more organized, and more women would get involved. But would it happen in her lifetime?

She'd finally found her niche in life. But with two loves—Deuce Jones, and coaching—she'd have to give up one. The decision kept her awake at night. Deuce would never be happy leaving Jinx Bay. That was a given. But would she ever be truly happy if she had to give up a dream job of coaching on the college level? She was good. College-level good. Everyone said so. And the temporary position at Troy had opened the door for amazing opportunities. Being considered for a head coaching position for women's basketball at Auburn University was a dream come true. This was much more than she could've ever hoped for, yet now it was about to become a real possibility.

Since there were very few female's vying for Coach's positions, Maddie dreamed of being on the cutting edge when the sport would finally gain the respect it deserved. If that should happen, and she had no doubt that one day it would, she'd need to be spending as much time as possible honing her skills.

But then there was Deuce. She covered her face with her hands and groaned. She and Deuce had planned an April wedding. Yet, he'd made it perfectly clear that a honeymoon would be put on hold, since fish bed in Spring and he couldn't possibly get away from his responsibilities at the Fish Camp. Maddie understood at the time. Or at least, she made an attempt to understand. Now, after receiving the letter from Auburn, everything she'd said previously about her willingness to be a PE teacher at a small county high school, in a little one-traffic-light fishing village, seemed grossly unfair. Why should she be forced to give up her dream in order for Deuce to realize his?

Whatever decision she made would need to come soon. In her heart she felt she'd already made her choice, although it was hard for her to admit it.

Maddie regretted that she'd had so little time to spend with her six-year-old niece, Tina, at the Troy Children's home, but her assistant coaching job had required a great deal of her time.

However, it wouldn't be long before basketball season would end, and she could visit more often. The fact that Tina appeared content at the Children's Home, helped expel some of the guilt feelings.

Deuce had said that once they were married, they'd get custody and raise Tina as their own child. He was so good with children she had no doubt that he'd make a great daddy. But was she ready to become a mommy? She thought so six months ago. But that was before she understood what she was capable of doing.

It wasn't that she didn't eventually want to have a family. But she was still young and had plenty of time. Why the rush? But what would Deuce say if she should tell him she wanted to hold off on marriage? Would he understand? Probably not. He was all about "a woman's place is in the home, cooking, cleaning, taking care of her man and raising a bunch of kids." Frankly, she'd thought the same way—that is, until the letter came from Auburn. Now, she was taking a different view of things.

She grabbed her purse and was ready to leave when someone knocked on the door. Maddie opened it, then squealed. "Josie! Is that really you?"

Josie grabbed her in a hug. "In the flesh. But I can see I've come at an inconvenient time. I knew I should've called, but I wanted to surprise you."

"Surprise me, you did. And no, it isn't an inconvenient time. In fact, it couldn't have been a better time. I need your advice, girlfriend. Come on in and have a seat. We have lots to talk about."

"Are you sure I'm not stopping you from something?"

"No, I was on my way to the Children's Home, but I can go anytime. Can I get you a glass of tea?"

"I'm fine. But won't Tina be expecting you?"

"She's fine. It's a great place. With all the kids around, she really doesn't have time to get lonesome. But tell me what you're doing here?"

"I'm on my way to Market in Atlanta, and since I had a little time to spare, I thought I'd drop by and see how things are going?"

"Good! Really good. But I want to know more about you and this business you're involved in."

"It's fabulous, girl. I get to pick out all the latest fashions for Gayfer's. It keeps me in beautiful clothes, since they encourage me to wear the samples." She stood and turned around. "How do you like it?"

"It's gorgeous, and so are you. I'm happy for you. How's Steve?"

Josie cackled. "Steve who?"

Maddie popped her palm over her mouth. "You're kidding? You two are no longer an item?"

"No. I won't deny I miss the big lug, but it was impossible to have a relationship, with him in one state and me in another. He's bought a big truck farm in Tennessee. I heard from a friend of his that he's about to tie the knot. But I want to hear more about the wedding."

"What wedding?"

"Yours, of course. Didn't you say it'll be in April?"

"Oh! Yes. April, that's right."

Josie's brow creased. "Hold on. Is there something you aren't telling me?"

"It's a long story."

"I have time if you do."

Maddie broke down in tears as she shared her dilemma. "I love him, Josie. Truly, I do. You may not believe that, and I'm sure Deuce won't believe it, either, if I call off the wedding. But it's the truth. I do still want to marry him. Just not now. I have the chance of a lifetime to do something that far exceeds anything I could've ever dreamed possible. All I want is a chance to prove I'm capable. Is that asking too much?"

"Maddie, I don't think anyone can answer that but you. Ask yourself the question. Which is more important? Deuce or Coaching?"

"That's the problem. I love them both. There's always the chance that I could lose Deuce if I put off the wedding in order to coach. However, I know in my heart that if I should get married and move to Jinx Bay, I'll die there with an apron on. I'll never get an opportunity like this again."

"Well, you've asked my advice, so here goes. Maddie, I don't think you're in love with Deuce. I know you think you are, but I don't see it."

"You can't be serious. That's crazy. I wouldn't be so stressed over making this decision if I didn't love him. Why would you even say such a thing?"

"I know you're sincere in believing that you do, and I'm not condemning you. Stop and think about it. You met him at a very vulnerable time in your life. You were running away from that Victor character, when Deuce and his father showed up in your life. Deuce immediately became your deliverer and freed you from fear. For the first time in months, you were able to breathe. I think you've confused being grateful with being in love."

"You're wrong, Josie. I know the difference in gratitude and love, but they go hand-in-hand. It's hard to separate the two."

"Okay, maybe I am wrong. It won't be the first time. I'm just telling you how it appears to me."

Deuce Jones was the kindest and the most lovable human being that Maddie had ever known. And yes, the night they met, she was exceedingly grateful to be the benefactor of his kindness, considering all she'd been through with Victor.

How does love ever to begin if not with a sense of gratitude? A woman meets a man and is *grateful* to learn he enjoys her company. Love grows.

Or two people are *grateful* to learn they have the same interests and decide they want to see more of one another. Love grows.

Or the woman meets a man who finds her attractive. She's *grateful,* because she wants to see more of him. From gratitude, love grows.

Maddie loved Deuce more than she'd ever loved a man, and

even if it had begun with a sense of gratitude, would that be so terrible? For as long as she had known Josie, Maddie had relied on her wise counsel. But Josie was wrong this time.

If she weren't in love with Deuce, then why would she be so concerned about his feelings? Why wouldn't she pick up the phone, call and say something to the effect that 'You're a nice guy and I've had fun with you, but something that I want more than you has come my way.' She couldn't do it. And why not? There could only be one answer. She loved him too much to want to hurt him.

"Josie, you question my love for Deuce, simply because I don't want to let go of a once-in-a-lifetime opportunity. Why do I have to be the one to give up my career to prove my love? No one expects Deuce to give up his job. Why don't the same rules apply?"

"I'm not saying they shouldn't apply, Maddie. But you need to be prepared for the outcome. You're already aware that he has no intention of leaving Jinx Bay.

So, let's turn the situation around. Suppose this opportunity hadn't come along for you, and you were looking forward to that Spring wedding. Then, suppose Deuce called to say an opportunity had come along that meant more to him than getting married, and that he'd give you a call in a year or two to let you know if he were still interested—what would you say?"

Maddie thought for a minute. "I hope I'd be happy for him that he had an opportunity to do something that meant a lot to him."

"Seriously? You wouldn't question his love?"

"I don't think so. No, I'm sure I wouldn't. I know he loves me, and I love him enough to want him to be happy."

"I think you're kidding yourself. But that's not the scenario you're facing, is it? The question is, does he love *you* enough to support your decision?"

Maddie shrugged. "I think so. Yeah. I'm sure he does. We have so much fun when we're together. He makes me laugh."

Josie raised a brow. "Red Skelton makes me laugh but I'm not in love with him."

Maddie picked up a pillow from the sofa and threw it at her. "You're being silly. It's not just because he's funny that I love him. I love him because—" She bit her lip. "Well, I love him, and he loves me for all the reasons two people ever fall in love."

"That's great. Since you're confident he loves you and would want you to follow your dream, it looks as if you have your answer. Call him and tell him your good news."

Maddie rubbed her hand over her mouth. "Well, I suppose if I were really sure he'd understand, we wouldn't be having this conversation, would we? What should I do, Josie? I don't want to lose him, but neither do I want to give up the opportunity of a lifetime."

"Let's evaluate both scenarios. If you choose to go forward with the wedding in April, you're saying that in all probability you'll never have another opportunity to coach college ball. Is that right?"

Maddie nodded. "True. But on the other hand, if Deuce loves me the way he says he does, then he should be happy for me and agree to wait until I can be recognized as a college-level coach."

Josie said, "Is that what you want to do?"

"I think so."

"I suppose if you postpone the wedding for two or three years, at the end of that time, you'll either both be ready to get married, or you will both have moved on."

"I just wonder how he'll take it when I tell him."

"He may be more accepting of the idea than you have imagined. From what you've told me, he has a lot of responsibility running a successful fishing industry. He may be trying to think of a way to tell you he needs more time."

"I hadn't thought of it like that, but you may be right. He's always writing about how busy he is, and how many hours he's putting in. The bookkeeper was hired before he took the job, and according to Deuce she can't put two figures together and come up with the right answer, so he's having to do his work and hers too."

"There you go. I know he loves you, Maddie, but stress can cause the best of marriages to collapse. I don't know about you, but when I tie the knot, I want it tied forever."

Maddie nodded. "I feel the same way."

Josie stood. "Well, I didn't mean to stay this long. I need to get on the road before dark. But I'm glad we had a chance to talk."

"Me too. Being able to talk through the situation with you has given me things to consider."

"If I helped in any way, I'm glad. Just don't make this more difficult than it has to be. I have no doubt that you'll make the right decision, but the longer you put it off, the harder it will be."

CHAPTER 8

After Josie left, Maddie looked at the clock. It was too late to visit Tina. She needed to be at the gym in less than an hour. She walked over to her desk, sat down and pulled out a sheet of stationary. Josie was right. Why put it off? Christmas was right around the corner. As busy as Deuce had been, she was sure he hadn't had time to buy her a gift yet, so the sooner she told him, the easier it would be for them both.

With pen in hand, she wrote:

My Dearest Deuce,

What I'm about to write has been a very difficult decision for me, but it's something I must do, for both our sakes.

Deuce, I love you very much. I hope you know that. I believe you love me, too. But I've done a lot of thinking lately, and I've concluded that we were too hasty in setting the wedding date for Spring.

We are both just beginning our lives as responsible adults, and as such, I'm afraid I wasn't acting in a very responsible manner when I suggested we marry so soon. You tried to tell me it was a bad time for you, since it's your busiest season, and now I find it's also a bad time for me.

Darling, I know you'll be happy for me when I tell you that I've received a letter from Auburn University, offering me an interview for a coaching position. You know this is more than I could've ever hoped for, yet it was dropped in my lap. I am beyond excited. Of course, I have no idea if I'll get the job, but the fact that they've offered me an interview is evidence that even if it doesn't pan out, my credentials are good. My chances of being considered by other major colleges have greatly improved.

It would be wrong of me to ask you to give up your job at Jinx Bay to follow me, and I'm sure you'd never ask me to give up something that I want so badly to move to a little fishing village, where everything I've worked for would be for nought.

Once we're established and have tried our wings, if we still feel marriage is right for us, then we'll figure it out.

Whatever our future holds, I wish you well, sweetheart, and I hope you wish the same for me.

Yours truly,

Maddie.

She read it over four times before folding it and placing in an envelope. A lump formed in her throat. It would break his heart, but she had to convince him it was the right thing for them both.

Wouldn't it be better to start a marriage with no regrets, than to rush into something and always wonder what could've been?

Maddie tossed and turned all night, too excited to sleep. She left Troy early in order to arrive in Auburn in time for her ten o'clock appointment. Working as the Assistant Coach at Troy had been a great experience, and a part of her heart would always belong to Troy State College. But just the thought of becoming the head coach of the Women's Basketball team at Auburn University made her head swim. Besides, she looked good in bright orange.

Deuce wouldn't understand, and the last thing she wanted was to hurt him, but this wasn't a decision she came to lightly. It was imperative that she stand firm and not allow him to sway her. Maddie's lip quivered. How many times does a girl get such an opportunity as the one that was literally thrown in her lap? If it were possible for her to coach and be married to Deuce, it would be fantastic. But that wasn't in the cards.

She knew Deuce well enough to know that he'd try to convince her that coaching a college women's basketball team would have no more prestige than coaching kickball at a grammar school. Maybe that's how folks viewed it at the present, but there were changes coming soon and coming fast.

He'd be very persuasive and encourage her not to give up on their plans for a Spring wedding. If he continued to insist, she'd need to be prepared. An idea popped in her head. She'd simply respond, "We'll still plan on a Spring wedding, if you're prepared to move to Auburn." It would put the ball in his court, so to speak, and there was no doubt the conversation would end there. No way would he agree to leave Jinx Bay. He needed to know her as well as she knew him, and if he did, he'd understand there was no way she could give up on her dream that was about to become real.

The day of the interview, she went to the Registrar's office in Auburn and was directed to Coach Weeks' office, located inside the Gym. Seeing the coach's name on the door, she knocked. Lightly at first, but when no one answered, she knocked once more, with a little more force.

One of the guys shooting baskets yelled, "She's gone."

"Gone? I have an appointment. Would you happen to know when she's expected to return?"

"Not really. I heard her say she had a family emergency. It must've been important because she left in a hurry."

"I see. I wonder why I wasn't informed in the Registrar's office?"

"Dunno. Maybe she didn't go by there."

"Thanks."

Disappointed, she left.

CHAPTER 9

By the time Deuce and Candy reached the Fish Camp, the rain was coming down in torrents, She pulled her convertible up near the storage room door and ran inside.

After spending time with Deuce at the restaurant, she was even more positive than ever that this was where she was supposed to be. She had thoroughly enjoyed listening to him tell about how he and the girl he plans to marry had met. He was so sweet. There was certainly nothing pretentious about him, which made him quite different from the men—mostly bankers—whom she'd surrounded herself with for the past few years. She hoped this Maddie person knew what a lucky girl she was.

Candy sat down in the swivel chair and pulled out the giant ledger from the desk drawer. She opened it up and rolled her eyes. It would be a challenge, for sure, but it wouldn't be the first challenge she had ever faced.

Deuce came rushing through the door of the storage room with his shirt soaked through and through. He laughed as he brushed his wet hair from his forehead.

He said, "The rain had slackened to a drizzle whenever I parked, but just as I stepped out of the truck, it seemed the bottom fell out and I got drenched."

Candy said, "I'm sure you want to run home to get on dry clothes, but if you have time to spare this afternoon and can go over the books with me, I'm ready to get to work."

"I do want to get out of these wet duds, and it looks as if the rain has stopped. You said you'd like to see the cabin. Would you be interested in riding over there with me now? You'll have a chance to see it while I run in and change."

She closed the ledger. "Sounds good. I'll need you to sit down with me when we get back, and let's talk about how we'd like to handle these over-charged accounts. I have a suggestion, but only if you think it's the best way to take care of it."

When they drove down a two-rut path surrounded on both sides by a dense forest with high underbrush, Candy decided that when Deuce referred to it as the cabin in the woods, he wasn't kidding. It was a cabin, not much larger than the cottages, and it was certainly in the woods.

She followed him inside. "I'll bet it's scary out here at night."

"Scary? I hadn't thought about it."

She laughed. "I know that town is not far away, yet it feels so far from civilization. I'm not putting it down. It's really quite homey looking. Just saying it would be very dark here at night."

She loved the way the twinkle in his eye seemed to dance when he smiled. His whole face lit up, as if he didn't have a care in the world. Candy wondered what that would feel like.

Deuce went into the bedroom and changed into a white undershirt. He walked out holding a long-sleeved shirt in his hand. Candy was surprised to see such a fine physique, which had been hiding beneath the loose flannel shirt.

He put on the shirt, then walked her out to the porch, where they sat down in the swing, and he gave her the cabin's history. He told her about how he grew up thinking his dad was killed in the war, when in fact he was hiding out there to keep his family from seeing what the war had done to his face.

Candy loved hearing him share the details. What an amazing life he'd had. She hadn't known until now that Deuce was not only the Operational Manager of the Fish Camp, but he was the son of the man who owned the whole conglomerate. Wow! What a surprise. Yet, he'd managed to stay humble. She admired that.

Candy wanted to know more about this unusual character and encouraged him to tell about his family, his friends, his childhood, and his aspirations. She was fascinated with the kind of life he'd lived. But the most intriguing was hearing him talk about how his family observed the holidays—especially Thanksgiving and Christmas.

He seemed almost childlike as he shared how his mother always prepared huge, delicious meals and would invite friends over. He told about his father's childhood friend, a man name Joel, and the struggles he went through before getting his life back on track. Candy was amazed at how forgiving these people were. But if they should hear about the things she'd done, could they find it in their hearts to forgive her? Why chance it?

The favorite part of Deuce's story was when he told about the woman he called Peggy, who had her Down Syndrome baby snatched away from her, and how her ex-husband, Joel had shown up at the Christmas Dinner last year, with the baby in his arms. Moisture welled up in Candy's eyes as he related the heartwarming story.

She twisted the emerald ring on her finger, as she silently recalled her own Christmas memories. A lump swelled in her throat as she remembered how Jack had made a quick stop to her penthouse on Christmas Eve last year on his way to a party with his banker friends. He was late and encouraged her to hurry and open the gift he gave her before he had to leave.

She had spent the last two Thanksgivings' and Christmas's alone in her apartment while Jack enjoyed the holidays with his parents and siblings. Looking back, she couldn't help wondering why he couldn't have taken her with him. After all, he was divorced. Would it have been so wrong?

It didn't take her long to figure out why she wasn't invited. Jack was ashamed of her. Not her appearance, not her personality, not her intellect, but ashamed of what he'd turned her into. She hadn't wanted to admit it before, but hadn't it become too evident to deny?

He loved showing her off to his banker buddies at seminars, as long as it was being held in a city far removed from Montgomery. She'd flown with him to the mountains, the Florida Keys, Hilton Head, and other beautiful places. But never had she been invited to accompany him to an event in Birmingham, Atlanta or Mobile, where bankers' wives who could actually have friends or family in Montgomery might be in attendance. He was ashamed of her because he knew what they were hiding. Would a man like Deuce have left her to spend Christmas alone?

The thought was ridiculous. Deuce would never have turned her into his mistress, so he'd have no reason to be ashamed.

Candy felt such a peace as she and Deuce sat in the swing, with it gently swaying back and forth.

He said, "I still find it hard to believe that someone with your qualifications showed up in Jinx Bay, but I'm mighty glad that you did. I'm sure I won't be able to keep you long, but I'll be very grateful if you can straighten out the books before you move on. I have confidence that working together, we can handle it."

She knew she should be the one to suggest getting back to work, but how she wished she could have one more day at the cabin in the woods. It was beginning to seem much less spooky and a lot more like a place to call home.

On the ride back, she said, "Deuce, do you mind if I ask you something?"

"I have no secrets."

"Good. I was just wondering if your girlfriend is planning to live with you in the cabin."

"No."

"Really? Why not?"

His lip curled. "Because we aren't married."

When she pressed her lips together, he said, "Hey, I embarrassed you. I'm sorry. I was trying to make a joke, but it wasn't very funny. I knew what you meant. But the answer is still no."

He waited for her to expound on her reason for asking, but when she didn't he said, "Why did you ask? Would you want to live out here in these scary woods?"

Her eyes twitched as she nodded. "I think I would."

He laughed. "Now, you're being the one to make a joke."

"No, I'm serious. I'll admit as we drove down the path with limbs coming at us from every side, I did imagine what it might feel like at night. But after sitting out here on the porch and looking around, the place is getting to me. I do think I could be happy out here."

"You're a very unusual young woman, Candy McCoy."

Her smile faded. "If you only knew."

"What does that mean?"

"Nothing. I was just rambling. We should get on back. I'm eager to get the accounts in that ledger straightened out."

On the trip back, she said, "Deuce, I think this job is going to be just what I've been praying for. But you need to get it out of your head that I'm only here to pass time until something else comes along. I wouldn't have taken the job if I hadn't felt it was exactly where I'm supposed to be."

Was she serious? The girl reeked of money. The thought that someone of her caliber could've been praying to work in a remote little corner of the world in a dingy office while living in a two-room shotgun cabin made him want to know her story. What was it that she wasn't telling him?

Red flags waved around in his head. Though he couldn't discern what bothered him most, it was evident that something fishy was going on at Boggy Bayou and it wasn't just in the water. He couldn't put his finger on it. What if she was running from the law? The thought was absurd. She was no criminal. So, why didn't he sit her down and demand that she tell him what she was up to?

He knew the answer. She would find the accusation offensive and rightly so. He couldn't afford to scare her away. She was a top-notch assistant, and he needed her. Not him, personally, but the business. He racked his brain. What was the mystery surrounding Candy McCoy?

He couldn't deny he felt drawn to her. What red-blooded American male wouldn't be? She was drop-dead gorgeous. But it wasn't her good looks that gave him the weird feeling that the girl needed this job more than the job needed her. Where were these thoughts coming from?

It wasn't sympathy. Candy had everything going for her.

Maybe it was admiration that someone with so much could settle for so little. That was it. He admired her. And why not? She was young, beautiful, rich, smart, and humble. How many times could one find so many admirable qualities in such a well put-together package?

Why push the envelope? He knew all he had to know. He needed a bookkeeper and now he had one. *Let it go, Deuce.*

CHAPTER 10

Eufaula, Alabama

Peggy Jinright would never be able to thank her friend, Ramona Jones, for insisting she put the past behind her and go back to work.

Peggy's life had been a series of broken promises and shattered dreams. Having been on the brink of suicide, the job with Garrison and Gunter had been exactly what she needed, though she didn't fully comprehend it at the time. Being busy had managed to help get her mind off the tragedy of having the hospital snatch her baby from her and going through the trauma of losing her husband Frank, shortly afterward, in an automobile accident.

She and her former husband, Joel Gunter, had been getting along much better than she ever imagined possible, when she agreed to work for him again.

It was proving to be very different from the years when she

worked for him before. Those were dark days before he got his life straightened out and became a law partner with Judge Garrison.

Joel Gunter was a different man in more ways than one. He was less combative, more caring, and certainly more trustworthy. In years past, she took anything he said with a grain of salt, but now if he said something, she could believe it was true. Sometimes she wondered what her life would've been like if he had made the change earlier—back before she became pregnant with his child.

There had been times when she wanted to tell him that little Joey was his—especially when he'd ask questions and show such an interest in her sweet little boy. She couldn't deny that she wouldn't have her baby with her today, if not for Joel's efforts. He and Judge Garrison did a thorough investigation and not only found Joey, but they were able to bring him home to her.

The moment that Joel laid him in her arms last Christmas, was the greatest gift she had ever or could ever receive. Didn't he have a right to know the truth? Or did he? Yet each time she came close to letting him know he was Joey's father, something would happen to change her mind. Would he be furious with her for not telling him sooner? Would he understand why she couldn't? What possible good come from telling him now? What difference would it make? None, whatsoever. Joey was her baby and her responsibility. She didn't need nor want to share him with anyone else.

Ramona Jones poked her head in the door. "Busy?"

Peggy smiled. "Not too busy for my sweet friend. Come on

in."

"Are you sure I'm not interrupting?"

"In fact, you've come at a good time. What brings you over to our side of town?"

"I've just come back from Montgomery and was driving by when I decided to stop and ask your opinion."

"About what?"

"I went Christmas shopping and had planned to pick up something for Deuce's girlfriend."

"How is Maddie? Is she enjoying her job, coaching?"

"I suppose so. We haven't seen much of her. She and Deuce both stay so busy, they hardly have time left for one another."

"That's too bad."

"Oh, I don't know about that. I'd rather they not spend so much time together. It'll give them an opportunity to discover how much they really care."

"So, what did you buy for her?"

"That's just the thing. I didn't buy her anything. Everything I picked up seemed either too personal, or too impersonal."

Peggy laughed. "Forgive me, but I'm not sure I can help you. Nothing in between comes to mind."

Ramona shrugged. "I know I'm probably putting too much emphasis on the gift. She'll probably never pick it up again after she opens it, regardless of what I buy."

"It sounds as if you two aren't getting along."

"No, it isn't that. I'm just saying I don't know what young

girls her age like. When I was twenty-two, I was a single mom, trying to take care of Deuce, and too busy to worry about material possessions. My entire life centered around him."

"Have you asked Deuce for suggestions?"

"Are you kidding? He stays so busy, I'll be surprised if he even remembers to buy her something himself. I declare that boy works from daylight 'til dawn." Ramona said, "I don't want to keep you from your work, but be thinking on it. And while I'm here, I'd like to invite you and Joel over for our annual Christmas dinner, if you both are free."

"I can't speak for Joel, but I'd love to come. I'll never forget what a wonderful time I had last year at your Christmas Dinner."

"Yes, I'll never forget the look on your face, when Joel came walking in the house holding your beautiful baby in his arms."

Tears came to Peggy's eyes. "It was truly a Christmas miracle that he and the Judge were not only able to find the Institution where the hospital had sent Joey, but that they were able to have him released in their care. I'll never have a Christmas gift to top that one, if I live to be a thousand. I still get chill bumps, just thinking about it."

"How is that little bundle of joy of yours doing?"

"Truthfully, Ramona, at this age he seems like any normal, sweet little rambunctious boy. He's amazed me at how quickly he can grasp things. It's so different from what I was led to believe by the clinical psychologist. When he was born, I was drilled on all the things Joey would be incapable of doing. I won't deny it was frightening. But why didn't they tell me all the wonderful things he could accomplish? There are times when I don't even think about him having Down Syndrome. Did you know he's walking now?"

"You're kidding! That's wonderful."

Peggy laughed. "Sometimes I wonder. Just kidding, of course, but he's even amazed the pediatrician. The little stinker is into everything." Her demeanor suddenly changed. "I'm very proud of all that Joey is capable of doing, but to be truthful, there are many nights I lay awake and in spite of all his accomplishments, I wonder what it'll be like when he gets older. Will the kids shun him? Will it make him sad when he realizes he's different? Will I be able to help him meet his potential?"

Ramona said, "Honey, don't borrow tomorrow's headaches. Enjoy today's blessings. If you'll think back, you'll realize yesterday's headache became today's blessing. And what God did once, He can do again."

CHAPTER 11

Being President of City Council was becoming more of a headache than Deuce could ever have anticipated. If it hadn't been for his mother's insistence, he would never have accepted the position. Why did he even mention it to her? But the bigger question was why did he bend under the pressure?

He didn't catch on in the beginning, but now he realized she still had high hopes of him going home to Rose Trellis in Eufaula and carrying on the Jones' legacy. She wouldn't be happy until he was presiding over every possible civic club, taking over the Merchants' Association, Chairing the School Board, serving as Chairman of the Deacons at church and becoming the CEO of Jones' Industries, which included, but not limited to, the Fish Camp at Jinx Bay. Maybe it was right for Daddy Theo, but Deuce wasn't cut out of that same elitest cloth. His mother undoubtedly thought if he'd accept the position as President of City Council even though it was in Jinx Bay, the experience could start him out on the right track. He'd become "somebody" in Jinx Bay, instead of just "that guy who runs the boats."

He loved his mother. She'd always been there for him. The only reason he accepted the City Council job was to make her proud of him. He supposed in some small way, he felt he owed her something. But couldn't he pay her some other way? He had no desire to be thought of as one of "the town fathers." All that notoriety could go to someone else. He'd be just as happy if no one outside the Fish Camp knew his name.

He looked at the clock. He'd hardly have time to pick up a bite to eat at Mildred's before it would be time for another meeting to discuss the Christmas Festival. He hated these meetings. Slapping his palm across his forehead, he realized he'd forgotten to ask the guys to go over to Cabin #3 and let Candy tell them where she wanted the new furniture placed. They had brought the old furniture over earlier that morning and stored it, but the furniture store didn't deliver the new until after lunch. He had intended to send another crew over to set it up for her, after it was delivered. Now, everyone was gone, and Candy would need the bed set up before nightfall. There was only one thing to do. He'd have to apologize and promise to have it all in place for her before she went to bed, because he had no idea how long the meeting would take.

He drove over to Candy's cottage, and she was sitting on the steps, as if she were waiting for him. After his explanation, he said,

"If Granny Noles shows up—and she will—it could be midnight before I get away."

"Not a problem. I didn't purchase that much furniture, since the rooms are small. You and I together can have it set up in no time. What time is your meeting?"

"Seven o'clock, but I need to be there a little early."

"Would you mind if I went with you? If Jinx Bay is going to be my home, I'd like to get involved in the civic affairs. Besides, I love Christmas, and I think it's wonderful that the town is planning to have such a grand celebration."

"Of course. I didn't think about the fact you might like to go. That's great. Do you know where City Hall is located?"

"No, but could we ride together? I'll take my car."

Deuce ran his hands through his hair. "Actually, I plan on dropping by at Mildred's Café for a chili dog before it starts. I'll have to woof it down, but I'm hungry."

"That sounds great. We'll run by for a quick bite to eat, go to the meeting, then on to the cottage. Then, when we're done setting up the furniture, I'll drive you back here to pick up your truck."

Deuce had an uneasy feeling, yet to refuse her could give her the idea he thought she was making inappropriate advances, which was not the case. So why did he feel as if he were sneaking around, doing something he had no business doing?

They walked outside and she tossed him the keys to her car.

He caught them and said, "Does this mean you want me to drive?"

"Do you mind?"

"No, but—"

"But what? Are you afraid your fiancé might find out and be jealous?"

"That's silly. She knows she has no reason to be jealous."

"Good. Then, let's go."

He got in, pushed the seat back to a comfortable position, cranked the car, then waited before putting it in reverse.

"What's wrong, Deuce?"

"I've changed my mind. I think I'll let you go on to Mildred's and I'll see you at City Hall. I have something I need to take care of."

She lowered her head. "I'm sorry. I put you on the spot. You could've just told me you didn't think it was a good idea to be seen together. I understand. I hope I didn't give you the wrong idea."

He looked away. "I don't know what you're talking about."

"I think you do. Just to set the record straight, I think you're a handsome, smart guy, Deuce Jones. You're sweet, generous, and your girl is lucky to have you wrapped around her little finger. But even with all your wonderful attributes, to me, you're just 'bossman.'" She laughed, mocking the crew at work who never called him anything other than bossman. "I had no romantic notions in mind when I suggested we ride over together. But I don't want to do anything that would make you uncomfortable."

He pulled a handkerchief from his pocket and wiped beads of

sweat gathered on his upper lip. "Uncomfortable? Why would it make me uncomfortable?"

"I don't know. Maybe I read you wrong. Sorry."

"Yes, you did. Apology accepted." The idea that Maddie would ever have reason to be jealous of Candy or any other woman was ludicrous. *Really?* Then why did his heart pound a little faster and his mouth feel as if it had been swabbed with a cotton ball when Candy said he was handsome? She called him sweet . . . generous, but it was when she said, "Your girl is lucky to have you wrapped around her little finger," that put a thought in his head that had no business being there. Was she suggesting—? Deuce tried to shake the silly notion. What difference would it make, even if she had been coming on to him? He had eyes for Maddie and only Maddie.

He glanced at his watch. "I suppose I should get on over to City Hall. The extra few minutes will allow me time to go over the notes from the last meeting."

"But what about that chili dog?"

"I'll survive. We'll swing by Mildred's when the meeting is over."

He put the car in reverse, turned it around and headed to City Hall.

CHAPTER 12

The conference room was packed when they arrived. Deuce called the meeting to order and introduced Candy to the group, explaining that she had recently moved to town, and was his new bookkeeper.

Abby Brown and Linda Macky, both eighteen, sat on the back row. Abby raised a brow, and they both giggled and whispered, as they eyed the new girl. Everyone in town knew they'd had a crush on Deuce from the first day he arrived. Linda raised her hand. "Excuse me, but I thought this meeting was for the citizens of Jinx Bay. Are you sure she'd be interested in what we have to say?"

Deuce glared, then snapped back. "Only if you say something interesting, Linda."

Granny Noles didn't raise her hand, nor did she wait for further comment. She quickly added, "Well, I heard your girlfriend was a pretty little thing, but I declare if she's not even lovelier than

I had her pictured. When y'all getting married, shug?"

She caught him off guard. "Uh, in the Spring, Granny. I believe the date is April 15th."

"Well, since that's when income taxes come due, you'll turn a bad day into a great day. Now there'll be something good to look forward to."

He loved Granny, but if he let her get the upper hand, he'd never get control of the meeting. Her sentences didn't seem to have periods, so it was difficult to ever find a place to stop her. But he wondered where Granny had a chance to see Maddie. He couldn't remember ever introducing them. Maybe it was while she worked at Mildred's, before she went off to school.

Deuce was pleasantly surprised to learn several committees had formed since they last met. He was thrilled to see the excitement and hear of the progress being made.

Marti Thompson was young, single, and teaching first graders at Jinx Bay Elementary. She introduced herself to Candy and asked if she'd be interested in helping with the children's Christmas Pageant.

Delighted at being included, Candy grabbed Marti's hands with both of hers. "Thank you. I was hoping I could be used somewhere and helping with a children's play would be my favorite thing to do. It'll be fun working with you."

"Can you sew?"

"I can and I'd love to help make costumes. I don't have a

sewing machine, but I'll go to Walton Beach and buy one after work tomorrow."

Deuce overheard the conversation, and again marveled that someone who apparently had as much money as she had would wind up in a secluded little fishing village, away from civilization. He was sure she could make a lot more money working in the city. But who was he to question why someone would choose to spend their life in the middle of the boondocks? It was a question his mother had asked him many times, and he'd never been able to explain it to her satisfaction. Yet, when you know, you know. And he knew all the reasons he stayed. But what was Candy's story?

Noting the time, Deuce tried to bring the meeting to a conclusion, but each time he attempted, someone would bring up a new question and the conversation would start anew, and he couldn't blame it on Granny, this time. He was grateful to see such enthusiasm and unity, but he was aware of how late it was getting and all that he needed to do before going home.

He said, "Your enthusiasm is gratifying, and I can't wait to see all these wonderful plans take shape. It's gonna be the best Christmas Festival of all time. But folks, it's late and some of us have to work tomorrow," which drew laughs.

He waited for the last person to leave the building, then walked outside and saw Candy sitting in the passenger side of her convertible. Several people had gathered around. Some of the guys were obviously admiring the car, and a few women were chatting with Candy as if she were some celebrity come to town.

He wished she would've sat under the wheel instead of acting as if they were joint owners of such a fancy automobile. He knew how it looked to everyone who saw it. It wouldn't have looked as conspicuous to the busybodies if he had merely caught a ride with her, but for them to see that she had turned the keys over to him—well, it could easily be misconstrued, even by those not prone to gossip.

Perhaps he was making much ado over nothing. He'd built it up in his mind. No one thought a thing about it. After all, he and Candy were co-workers, and it was understandable that they would've decided to come together instead of on two separate vehicles.

He walked over and opened the door. George Taylor slapped him on the back. "Can't blame you, my friend. No sir. Don't blame you at all."

"Excuse me?"

George turned and winked at Bob, as if they shared a very amusing secret.

Aubrey Satterwhite seemed to be admiring more than the automobile. He was over on the passenger side, leaning in toward Candy. He grinned as if he'd won the lottery. Candy returned his smile. What were they discussing that was so amusing?

Deuce bristled seeing Aubrey lay his hand on the edge of the window, only a fraction of an inch away from Candy's' shoulder. His pulse raced. Where were these weird feelings coming from? He had no hold on Candy McCoy. Why should he care if Aubrey was flirting with her? Could he blame him? She was beautiful. In fact, if he didn't already have a girl—

He cranked the car and backed out of the parking lot. She said, "What's wrong?"

"Nothing. Why would you ask?"

"I don't know. You act as if something's bothering you."

He feigned a smile. "You're imagining things."

Candy said, "I know it's later than you anticipated. I hate for you to have to go put up my furniture at this hour, and if it weren't for not having a bed to sleep on tonight, I'd say forget it and send a couple of guys over tomorrow to set it all up."

"It's okay. We'll get it done tonight."

"I have a better idea. How comfortable is your sofa?"

His brow creased. "Why?"

"I was just thinking I could sleep on your sofa for one night. To tell the truth, I'm bushed. It has been a busy day."

His throat tightened. "I don't think that's a good idea."

"What are you afraid of?"

"I'm not afraid of anything. I just don't think it's a good idea."

She laughed. "You *are* afraid."

"Am not." The way she laughed at him made him feel like a kid. He lifted a shoulder in a shrug. "I'll take the sofa, and you can have the bed."

"Suit yourself but stop by the cottage and let me pack a bag."

"Why do you need a bag? You can drive back to your cottage early in the morning and dress there."

"I suppose you're right. I only wanted to pick up something to wear to bed, but I don't guess I need it for one night."

Deuce made no comment but turned down Cannery Road and stopped at Cottage #3.

She giggled. "I'll only be a minute."

He opened his door.

Candy said, "No need for you to get out."

"We might as well put your bed together while we're here. The guys can come tomorrow and finish setting up."

"But I thought—"

"No, Candy. I don't think you did."

In less than thirty minutes, the bed was set up, complete with bed linens.

Deuce drove back to his little cabin in the woods, where his father had spent years in hiding before having plastic surgery on his mangled face. Deuce had added an indoor bathroom and updated the kitchen, but other than that, it was still the same crude-looking little log cabin where he and Maddie went with his father, the first night he met her.

He undressed for bed, but in spite of being totally exhausted, he found it difficult to go to sleep. So many questions swarmed in his head. What if he'd brought Candy here? Was he only imagining that she was coming on to him, or was she really so innocent, she didn't realize how her suggestions caused his mind to wander down paths it had no business going? What if?

He sucked in a heavy breath of air, then expelled in a low

whistle. Maybe it was not such a good idea to move the bookkeeper's desk back into his office. Too late now. If only Maddie were here. He counted up the days before she'd be through with basketball practices before Christmas break.

Oh, Maddie, I miss you so much. I'd marry you tonight if you were here. You're all I want. All I'll ever want. I don't long for fancy cars or . . . or Candy McCoy, or— His pulse raced. Why did Candy's name pop in his mind if he hadn't longed for her? Unable to sleep, he got up, went into the kitchen, and took an aspirin, hoping it would make him sleep and he'd wake up in the morning with a clear mind. At least he took her home, so he could awake with no regrets, and that was a good thing. *The quicker Spring gets here the better I'll like it.*

CHAPTER 13

Back in Eufaula, Alabama . . .

At five o'clock, Peggy Jinright put the cover on her typewriter, walked into Joel's office to let him know she'd be leaving for the day.

He smiled. She'd never noticed what beautiful teeth he had. In fact, there were a lot of things about Joel Gunter she'd never noticed until recently. But then she realized she'd never really seen him flash such a genuine smile. The thought ran through her head that what he needed was a good woman in his life. She even had one in mind. Darla Grady was the Power of Attorney for an elderly relative. A client of the firm. She was about Joel's age, although she looked much younger. An astute businesswoman, she'd told Peggy she'd been too involved in promoting her business during her younger days, and now that she would soon be forty, all the good men were taken. Eighteen months ago, Peggy would've agreed with her. But after working with Joel this past year, she could honestly say there were still some fine, honest, middle-aged men left in the world. She smiled, as she anticipated ways to get the two together.

Joel said, "I'll walk you out. I have a little something in my car that I bought for Joey."

Peggy's brow lifted. "For Joey? But it's not his birthday."

"I know, but now that he's learned to walk, I think he'll love it." He opened the trunk of his car and pulled out a push-pull toy that made a terribly annoying sound when pushed along. Joel laughed seeing the cringe on Peggy's face. He said, "It's called a popcorn popper. Would you mind if I closed up and rode with you to the babysitter's, so I can see him when you give it to him?"

"I have a better idea. I put a roast in the oven when I went home for lunch and set the timer. Why don't you give me about thirty minutes, then come over and have supper with us?"

"Are you sure?"

"Of course. Joey and I both would count it an honor. I'll toss a salad, and cut up a few potatoes and while they're frying, you can teach Joey how to maneuver his new toy. But let me warn you—don't be disappointed if he pays it no attention and chooses to play with the bag it came in, instead. Every time I think I've found the perfect stimulus toy, I discover it's much more entertaining to me than it is to him."

"That sounds good. I'll see you about six o'clock?"

"Perfect."

Driving over to the sitters' Peggy thought it weird that her heart hammered, her palms felt sweaty, and she was singing an old love song she hadn't heard in years. Why was she feeling so goofy? It wasn't a date. Dating was the furthest thing from her mind, but even if she were entertaining such a crazy idea—which she wasn't—she certainly wouldn't be dating Joel Gunter. Heaven forbid. She'd been there, done that. Besides, romance was not something she and little Joey needed in their lives. Now or ever. They had one another and had no time for anyone else.

He was just coming over to give Joey a little something he picked up at Woolworth's, for crying out loud. Why was she acting like a schoolgirl who'd just been invited to the Prom? Could it be she was interested in Joel Gunter . . . as in romantically interested? She rolled her eyes. Ridiculous. She would be having that same reaction if the milkman had asked to come over. Or the old lady who ran the register at the meat market. She stopped in front of the house and walked down the sidewalk. "I've been alone so long, just the thought of having someone to sit down and share a meal with is exciting."

A woman walked past. "Were you addressing me?"

Peggy felt her face blush. "No. Sorry. I was mumbling to myself."

Joey saw her walk in and threw down his toy. The smile on his face lit up her heart. She thought back to when he was born and the psychologist at the hospital insisted she and Frank place Joey in an institution. It made her shudder, just thinking about how close she came to never seeing that little beautiful smiling face.

When she picked him up and asked for kisses, that precious little tongue wet the side of her face as he rubbed his mouth against her cheek. It always made her laugh. Nothing had ever felt as sweet as Joey's sloppy kisses.

Mrs. Taunton, the babysitter had raised nine children of her own. That was one of the reasons Peggy chose her. She figured most anything a child could go through would not be anything unfamiliar to someone who had birthed that many babies. Mrs. Taunton was a jolly old soul, and her love for children was evident, but sometimes Peggy felt she was being overly cautious with Joey.

Perhaps it shouldn't have bothered her, but the day that Joel laid Joey in her arms last Christmas, she made up her mind that she'd never treat him as if he were abnormal, because he wasn't. He was as normal as any other baby boy his age. Children are born with different color hair, different eye shapes, different personalities, and different kinds of normal.

Peggy wanted the babysitter to treat him the same as the other children, yet it seemed she was constantly having to try to ease Mrs. Taunton's fears. There seemed to always be something she was looking to fret over. She'd commented more than once about the bluish color in Joey's fingernails. Peggy tried to ease her unfounded fears. "They aren't blue, Mrs. Taunton. Perhaps not as pink as when he was younger, but it's nothing to worry about."

"It just doesn't look right to me, but I reckon if it was very concerning, your pediatrician would've let you know."

"Yes ma'am." Peggy made a point not to tell her she didn't believe in taking Joey into a doctor's office to sit among a roomful of sick children. As long as he was doing as well as he was, there was no need in taking chances. He was seldom sick, and when he was, she'd been able to nurse him back to health. One time in the past year he had a bout with diarrhea, but her friend Ramona had given her great advice, and by the end of the day, he was fine. Naturally, if something out of the ordinary were to come up, she wouldn't hesitate to seek medical treatment.

She supposed since Mrs. Taunton had never had a Down Syndrome child, she tended to look for ailments in Joey that she naturally overlooked in other children.

After Peggy strapped Joey in the car seat, she picked up his little hand and examined his fingernails. "Perfect!" Smiling, she lifted his hand to her lips and kissed all five stubby little fingers.

CHAPTER 14

Peggy barely had time to change Joey, put him in his playpen and set the table before she heard Joel drive up. She'd hoped to have time to at least brush through her hair and dot a little lipstick on her lips, but there was no time. She hurried into the kitchen and heard the front door open. She grabbed the platter of roast beef and took it into the dining room and placed it on the table.

Joel strode in and yelled, "Honey, I'm home."

Her face flushed. "What? What did you say?"

He laughed. "I wish you could see your face. I thought you'd think it was funny, but you look like someone facing the gallows."

"Don't be silly. I knew you were being goofy, trying to get a rise out of me. I did think it was funny." If he only knew what she was thinking. The really funny part was the fact that Joel Gunter had made a joke. She'd known him a long time, and a sense of humor had never been one of his character traits.

He bent down over the platter of meat and sniffed. "Say, that roast smells good. Thanks for inviting me over, Peg. It'll be good to get a homecooked meal."

Joey sat up in the playpen and held up his arms to be held. Joel said, "Do you mind if I pick him up?"

"I'm sure he'd love you forever. Now that he's walking, he doesn't like being cooped up."

"Seems he's awfully young to be walking."

"He's been walking for almost two months, and yes his pediatrician said most Down Syndrome children walk somewhere between eighteen and twenty-eight months, so I hadn't expected it quite so soon."

Peggy's pulse raced, when Joel picked him up and tossed him in the air, causing Joey to giggle uncontrollably. "Be careful, Joel."

"You just finish cooking little mama and let us have a little fun." He tossed Joey in the air once more and laughed with him. "He loves it, don't you, Buddy."

Peggy stood over the stove, keeping check on the rolls. She didn't like the feelings she was having. She'd been fooled once by Joel Gunter. She was too smart to be taken in twice.

When she called Joel to the table, he placed little Joey in the highchair beside him, but Joey cried as he leaned over toward Joel, holding out his arms.

When Joel reached for him, Peggy said, "No. I'll get him."

For once, they both seemed to find it difficult to find something to talk about. Peggy surmised it was because they were together eight hours a day and had already said anything that needed to be said. But the quiet was making her nervous. What did she expect by inviting him over? It was a stupid thing to do.

Joel said, "The rolls are good. Did you make them yourself?"

"No. They're Brown and Serve. I bought them at the Piggly Wiggly. Are you trying to flatter me by making me think this is the first time you've ever had Brown and Serve rolls?"

His face turned red. He ignored her comment, and mumbled, "They're good, whatever they are."

She felt her sarcastic comment had been uncalled for. Why was she being so mean? He'd done nothing but respond to her invitation to join her for dinner. If that was wrong, it was her own fault. Not his.

Joey had gone to sleep with his head on her shoulder.

Joel said, "Would you like for me to put him in his crib for you?"

"Thanks."

He walked over and gently picked up the baby and took him to the nursery. He came back to the table and sat down.

Peggy said, "That was kind of you." Attempting to lighten the mood to make up for her earlier snarky comeback, she thought she'd bring up Darla Grady's name. "Joel, I know you've been busy this past year, getting established again, but I've had something I've wanted to ask you. Have you considered dating?"

He was about to take a swallow of tea but sat his glass down. "Why? Have *you*?"

"Me? Heavens, no."

He looked down at his plate and cut his roast beef. "Same answer here."

After several uncomfortable minutes, Joel finally broke the silence. "Why did you ask?"

"Ask what?"

"What? You asked if I wanted to date. What prompted that question?"

"Oh. That. I thought if you were ready, I know someone who'd be perfect for you. She's beautiful, smart, owns her own business, is about our age and she's never been married."

He laid down his fork, picked up his napkin from his lap and laid it across his plate. He quickly shoved his chair away from the table.

Peggy said, "You aren't finished, are you?"

"Yes, thank you. I've had enough."

"I don't think you know her. I think you and Darla—"

His brow formed a vee. "Since I just told you I'm not interested in dating, I don't see why it's necessary that you pick out someone for me."

"You don't have to get angry."

"I'm not angry. I'm just saying I'm not interested in dating. Is that so hard to understand? Besides, you've said the same thing. Wouldn't it be a little ridiculous for me to try to fix you up with someone, knowing you've already made it clear that you aren't looking for a relationship?"

"You still sound irritated."

"Well, maybe I am. If and when I ever do decide to date again, I'm quite capable of picking out my own girlfriends." He made a point to look at his watch. "I suppose I should go. I have some errands to run. Thanks for dinner."

CHAPTER 15

Tuesday morning, Candy stopped by Deuce's office as soon as she arrived for work. "Just wanted to let you know I'm here and on time, bossman."

Rolling his eyes, he said, "I wish you wouldn't call me that."

"I think it's cute. I love hearing the guys refer to you in such an affectionate term."

"Affectionate? I'm not looking for their affection."

"You're too sensitive, Deuce. You seem to constantly be trying to second-guess everyone's motives, but there are times when you've been way off base."

"I'll admit I don't always get it right."

"I know."

"What does that mean?"

"I was just agreeing with you. No one gets everything right all of the time. I'd like for you to take a look at the Langston account and see if you approve of the way I've handled it."

Standing behind her, he leaned over her chair, as she pointed out specific areas where she had discovered discrepancies, then handed him the letter she had written to them.

But Deuce found it hard to concentrate on what she was saying, for sniffing her hair.

She turned around, looked up at him and laughed. "Do you have a cold?"

"No. Why?"

"Then are you sniffing me?"

He stammered. "Uh, sorry."

"You mean you really were smelling me?"

"Not you. The perfume in your hair . . . it . . .it smells good. What's it called?"

She snickered. "It's called Prell Shampoo."

Humiliated that she'd caught him, he straightened and read the letter. "Sounds good. Now, go tell Dan and Paul to take my truck and go over to your cottage and set up the remainder of your furniture. You'll need to drive your car over to show them where you want everything. When you get back, you can finish the payroll. If you have any questions, don't hesitate to come ask."

"I don't anticipate a problem. You were very thorough in your instructions." She was holding a handful of letters.

She said, "I brought the mail in, and I'll answer all the correspondence, except for this one." She threw a pink envelope on his desk. "It's marked personal. Your fiancé, I presume?"

He picked it up and smiled. "Yep." He ran it by his nose. "I could be blind and know it was from her. It's her White Shoulders."

"What?" She giggled. "So, she has white shoulders, does she? Interesting! Is that what first drew her to you?"

"Not her! Her fragrance." He handed the envelope back to her. "Sniff it."

Candy held it to her nose and sniffed. Not once, not twice but four or five times.

Deuce laughed. "It only takes once. You sound like a dog sniffing a bone."

"I don't smell a thing. What is it with you and your nose? You're smelling what you want to smell." She laid the letter on the desk.

He suddenly found it offensive that she'd poked fun at him.

Deuce grabbed the envelope, then holding it to his nose, he sucked in a heavy breath through his nostrils. "There's something wrong with your smeller if you can't smell this."

"Whatever you say, bossman. I'll go find Dan and Paul I can see you're chomping at the bits to find out what's in that envelope besides an imaginary perfume, bearing the peculiar name of a woman's anatomy. I think I'll invent something called Red Hot Lips. That sounds much more alluring, than White Shoulders, don't you think?."

Rolling his eyes, he said, "Can I help it if you have a defective nose?"

Deuce waited for her to close the door. Holding the envelope to his nose once more, he sniffed. Then again. And again. Was she right? Was it his imagination? He took the letter out unfolded it, then leaned back in his chair to absorb the contents:

What I'm about to write has been a very difficult decision for me, but it's something I must do, for both our sakes.

Deuce, I love you very much. I hope you know that. I believe you love me, too. But I've done a lot of thinking lately, and I've concluded that we were too hasty in setting the wedding date for Spring.

"What?" He mumbled, "Maddie wants to call off the wedding? Why? What have I done?"

He picked up the phone to call her. "I'd like to make a long-distance call, please. Person to Person. I'm calling—" He slammed the phone down and decided to finish reading her letter.

He started with the next paragraph:

We are both just beginning our lives as responsible adults, and as such, I'm afraid I wasn't acting in a responsible manner when I suggested we marry so soon. You tried to tell me it was a bad time for you, since it's your busiest season, and now I find it's also a bad time for me.

He wadded the letter without finishing it and threw it in the trash. "You're right Maddie Anderson. It's a very bad time for me to get married. Let me take a look at my calendar. Hmm . . . now that I think about it, it doesn't look as if there'll ever be a good time for me to marry you."

Deuce found it impossible to finish a single project all morning. He wasn't sure if he was grieving over her breaking up with him because he loved her and wanted to be with her— or if it was a mere matter of his hurt pride at being dumped.

At lunch, Candy came by his office. "The fellows did a great job setting up everything for me. I haven't had a chance to buy groceries, or I'd invite you over for lunch to celebrate my moving in. But I'd love to take you to Mildred's for her blue-light special, as a thank you for all you've done to get me settled in."

"Thanks, but I'm not particularly hungry. I'll probably stay here and—" He stopped. "No. I've changed my mind. I will go with you. Besides, today is corned beef and cabbage day. I could use a good meal. Let's go."

"Your truck or my car?"

"Let me take you."

Once they got to the diner, and sat down, Candy said, "Okay, now tell me."

"Tell you what?"

"What has you so upset. You didn't say a word all the way here. Did I do something to upset you?"

"You? Of course not. It has nothing to do with you."

"Then forgive me for being nosey."

"I haven't considered you nosey. It's just not something I want to talk about." Candy changed the subject and began telling him all the plans that she and Marti had made to get ready for the Children's Christmas Pageant. "She's invited me to go to church with her Sunday and visit her Sunday School class. She teaches First thru Third Graders, and it will give me an idea about sizes for costumes. Oh, Deuce, I'm so excited. This is going to be so much fun."

Deuce tried to at least pretend to be interested in the conversation, but it was difficult trying to keep up with what Candy was saying, while going over in his mind what could've made Maddie stop loving him.

"That's nice," he commented, hoping it was a sensible response to what she'd just said.

She stopped. "What's wrong, Deuce?"

"I said I don't want to talk about it."

"Okay, I'm sorry. Are you going home for Thanksgiving?"

"What?"

"Thanksgiving. I asked if you'll be going to Eufaula?"

"I hadn't thought about it, but yes, I suppose I will. My mother will be counting on it. What about you? Going home?"

"Yes, I plan to leave tomorrow after work. You did say we have Thursday and Friday off. Right?"

"That's right. The office will be closed. I haven't thought to ask. Where is your home?"

"Tampa."

"That'll be quite a trip."

"It's not so bad."

"Tell me about your family."

"Oh, they're the best. Daddy is a banker, and Mom stays busy with all the charities she's involved with."

"Brothers and sisters?"

She shook her head. "No, I'm an only child. I guess you can tell my Daddy spoils me, but he says, 'What else will I do with my money, if I don't spend it on you, Punkin.'" Tears welled in her eyes as she spoke of her father. "That's his pet name for me. Sounds childish, but it's sweet the way he says it."

"I can tell you love him very much."

"More than you can imagine. What about you?"

"Same here. . . only child, and I'd be happy with a little less attention. Mom is swell, but she doesn't want to let go of the apron strings, if you know what I mean."

"Then you understand how important it is to our parents to have us home on special holidays."

"Absolutely." Deuce picked up the bill, then pulled out his wallet.

Candy said, "Please let me pay. After all, I invited you out. I'll feel better if you'll let me."

"I wouldn't feel right about it."

"Well, at least allow me to pay for my own. That way, I won't feel bad about coming with you on more lunch dates if you'll let me take care of my own bill."

He picked up a dollar-fifty from the table. "If you insist, but I don't mind paying."

On the way back to work, she said, "Deuce, I hope you didn't take offense when I called our little outing a lunch date. I didn't mean to infer we were dating. I just meant—"

"Skip it Candy. I know what you meant."

CHAPTER 16

Troy, Alabama

Mattie walked into her apartment, hot, tired, and very thirsty. Today, she questioned her insistence that her girls be allowed to play full court. They were on their game today, and she could hardly keep up with them.

After gulping down two large glasses of water, she picked up the phone several times with the intention of calling Deuce. Satisfied that he'd had time to receive her letter, she couldn't understand why he hadn't bothered to respond. She had expected a phone call upon receipt of the news, but when the call didn't come, she figured he couldn't bring himself to talk with her. She checked her mailbox daily, and concluded that by this time, he'd had ample time to respond by mail.

A knot formed in her throat. He was devastated, as she knew he would be. But if only he'd call she could explain they both had dreams and neither of them were willing to give up on something that meant so much, nor should they be expected to. Surely, he could understand, even if he wished it could be some other way. She'd tell him how she admired him for the way he went after what made him happy. She'd plead with him to understand that her dreams were as important to her as his was to him. How could that be so hard to understand?

Mattie stayed by her phone as much as possible, waiting for the call that never came. Although she'd counted on Deuce picking up the phone as soon as he opened her mail, she decided he was doing the right thing by taking his time to respond. It would be too easy for either of them to say something out of hurt, anger, bitterness or even love that they might later regret.

Maddie soon faced facts and decided he had no intention of calling. Although a bit surprised she was okay with that. She was better than okay. It would be much easier on them both to say their goodbyes through letters. If he broke down over the phone, she wouldn't be strong enough to stand up to him and would likely give in against her better judgment. That would be wrong. Not only for her sake, but for his also. No, she had to stand firm. He was hurt. She knew he would be. But she had hoped he'd allow her the opportunity to explain her reasons for breaking up, which she'd found too difficult to express on paper.

Feeling she was spending far too much time dwelling on something that couldn't be fixed, she rode over to The Children's

Home to visit Tina. When she drove up, Tina and two of her little friends came running over to the car.

Tina's first words were, "What did you bring me?"

Maddie bit her lip. She'd made it a habit of taking something to her little niece on every trip, but her mind had been so preoccupied with Deuce, she'd allowed everything else to slip her mind. She said, "What if I asked permission to take you three girls to Whopper Burger for an ice cream?"

Hearing their squeals of delight was evidence she was forgiven.

While inside enjoying their treats, Tina said, "Aunt Maddie, the housemother said I could invite you to have Thanksgiving Dinner with us, but I told her you'd probably want to take me to your apartment to spend Thanksgiving."

Jackie said, "My grandparents are coming to get me, and I get to spend three whole days at their house."

The other child said her Daddy and stepmother would pick her up on Thanksgiving Day, then added, "But I don't get to spend the night. Daddy says they'll be too busy Friday to bring me back to the Children's Home, but I can have lunch with them."

Tina said, "Can you cook a turkey, Aunt Maddie?"

Maddie had her mind on other things and had paid little attention to the conversation taking place. Tina repeated. "Can you, Aunt Maddie?"

"I'm sorry, sweetheart. What is it you want to know?"

"What are you and I having for Thanksgiving dinner? Can you

cook a turkey?"

"A turkey? No way. Why?"

"Then what will we eat?"

It suddenly dawned on Maddie that her little niece had the idea they'd be spending the day together. Did the housemother put that into her head? Then again, maybe she assumed it on her own, since her little friends would be spending time with their families. Maddie was the only family Tina had, except for her father, who was serving time in prison. An idea popped in her head. She'd save it until after she took the other kids back to the Home.

When the girls jumped out, Maddie asked Tina to wait. "How would you like to go see your daddy on Thanksgiving Day?"

Her eyes widened. "Do you mean it?"

"Of course, I mean it."

"But how would I get there?"

"I'll take you. I'd like to see him, too. He's my big brother."

Tina grabbed her around the neck and squeezed. "Thank you, Aunt Tina. I love my daddy. I didn't think I'd ever see him again."

"I'll go inside with you to let the housemother know that I'll pick you up tomorrow. You can spend the night with me, and we'll leave early on Thanksgiving Day."

CHAPTER 17

Back in Eufaula . . .

Ramona sat across the table from her husband at Andy's Steakhouse, while waiting for their friend Joel to join them. She said, "Honey, do you think Deuce will ever come back home?"

He laughed. "What brought that up?"

"I was just thinking how senseless it is for him to be wasting his time running the Fish Camp and Cannery when he could be such an asset to the town of Eufaula."

"Are you saying he's not an asset to Jinx Bay?"

"Pooh. There's no one there who can even spell the word asset, much less know what it means. That son of ours has a head on his shoulders. He could be making a difference here."

"Ramona. Give it up. Deuce is making a difference right where he is. I don't know why you keep harping on getting him to come back home, when he's told you he's perfectly happy where he is."

"Oh, Ronald, he's living a pipe dream, and you know it. By the time it blows up in smoke, it'll be too late for him. He needs to start now, making a name for himself. Your father handed down a great life for you and Deuce. I've been proud of how you have taken over where Daddy Theo left off, but who is gonna carry on your legacy when you're gone, if Deuce doesn't come back and get himself known in the circles."

"Circles? Circles of society, you mean. Well, honey, I've tried to explain this to you before, but you don't seem to want to listen, so I see no reason to go into it again."

She rolled her eyes. "There's Joel, coming in the door. I was hoping you'd understand what I was trying to tell you, but obviously you've closed your mind to it and are willing to let Deuce make a terrible mistake that I'm afraid he'll live to regret."

Joel walked up. "I hope that conversation was not about me, although since it was about someone's mistake, it certainly could apply here."

Ramona smiled. "Not about you at all, Joel. Ronald and I both are very proud of how you turned your life around and are doing so well."

"Thanks. I've seen both sides of life, and I'll tell you the truth. Becoming homeless will certainly humble a person. I have much more compassion for the down-and-out than I ever did before. I once hee-hawed at lawyers who'd take a pro bono case. I no longer laugh. In fact, I'm working on one at the moment that takes more of my time than the others, yet I find it very gratifying. But enough about me. When have you heard from that son of yours?"

Ronald said, "He talked to Ramona one day last week. He's still loving it."

"I heard he was engaged."

Ramona said, "Yes. Maddie is a lovely girl. She's an Assistant Women's Basketball Coach at Troy State College."

"Wow. That sounds great, but you look as if you have reservations."

"We like her a lot, but I do wish they would've waited a couple of years before planning a wedding. Deuce needs more time to get established before taking on so much responsibility."

Joel smiled. "Well, with two incomes and no dependents, I'm sure they'll fair fine."

"That's just the thing. They won't have two incomes. She'll have to give up her job when they marry. And that's not all. She has a little niece at The Children's Home in Troy, and although she hasn't said it outright, I have a strong feeling she's planning to adopt her as soon as she and Deuce marry. Starting out that way, they're likely to struggle for the rest of their lives."

Ronald chuckled. "Ramona has them on Welfare, already. Looks like you may have another pro bono case, Joel, when they start the adoption process."

Ramona's jaw flexed. "It's nothing to joke about Ronald Jones. I'm concerned about them making a mistake that could affect their lives for a very long time, when it could easily be avoided by holding off on getting married until they get established."

Joel held up both palms. "I'm staying out of this conversation. I can see it's a sore spot."

Ramona said, "We've talked about Deuce's love life, but what about yours, Joel?"

He held his head back and cackled. "What love life? At my age, I've thrown in the towel. Besides, I'm too busy for such foolishness."

"Foolishness? Who are you trying to kid? Seriously, now that you've got so much going for you, you need to take time out to find a good woman to share your life with."

"And where will I find that good woman, Ramona? The ones I come in contact with at work, all come with baggage that I don't need."

"What about at church?"

He raised a brow. "We go to the same church. Have you seen someone there you think I need to propose to?"

"You're making fun of me."

"Not making fun. Just being realistic."

"Well, I know there's a lovely lady somewhere that the Lord has picked out for you. You just need to keep your eyes and mind open, so you'll recognize she's the one." Ramona wanted to blurt out Peggy's name, but afraid that he'd nix it to begin with, which could keep him from ever considering her again, she decided it was best to let him think of it for himself.

Joel smiled. "Well, if you find her before I do, would you please give her my phone number?"

Ramona's eyes opened wide. "So, you are ready for a relationship?"

Ronald said, "For crying out loud, sweetheart, would you stop badgering him? He's a grown man and I'm sure when he's ready, he's capable of finding his own woman."

She frowned. "His own woman? You make him sound like a cave man. I just pictured him pulling a woman into his cave by her hair."

Joel laughed. "What did she look like?"

"I beg your pardon?"

"You said you pictured her. Was she blond, brunette? I'm trying to get that same picture in my head."

She blew out a puff of air. "I declare, you two are impossible. I see I'll need to take care of this matter with no help from either of you. But you may be surprised. She could be within your grasp, and if you aren't paying attention, she could slip right from your fingers into someone else's' arms."

Ronald shook his head. "As you can see, Joel, my wife is quite the romantic and unless you want her picking out a wife for you, I'd say you'd better start looking for yourself."

"I don't think I've made myself clear. The last thing I need in my life is a wife."

CHAPTER18

The ladies in charge of setting up the Bakery Booth for the Jinx Bay Christmas Festival met at the home of Phyllis Crawford. Phyllis had baked a Lemon Cheesecake to serve for refreshments.

The Bakery Committee was one of the smaller committees, and Deuce presumed it was because not many women were willing to be on a committee with Granny Noles. She could be headstrong when she wanted to be, and more times than not, she wanted to be.

The spinster sisters, Daisy and Dixie Austin were the first to arrive. Then Lula, Oleta, and Frannie arrived. Phyllis greeted them, and mentioned wondering where Granny Noles was, since she was always the first to arrive at any of the meetings.

Oleta said, "I'll go ahead and call the meeting to order, and we can enjoy Phyllis's delicious refreshments as we hash out our business." Phyllis served the cake, nuts, and cheese straws on pretty dessert plates as the ladies stayed seated.

"I suppose to begin with we need to decide what all we wish

to sell. This lemon cheesecake of Phyllis' will definitely go quickly."

Oleta said, "And the Austin twins make the best fruit cake I've ever eaten, and I've had a lot of fruit cakes in my time. Dixie said, Daisy gets all the praise. She took Mama's recipe and tweaked it, and folks sure seem to enjoy it."

Daisy blushed. "It's simple, really, I leave out a lot of the candied fruit that the original recipe called for and add more nuts. But sister and I delight in making it every Christmas and we get a thrill out of seeing folks enjoying it."

Frannie said, "I love the taste of the fruit cake batter, but so many of the recipes have too much candied fruit in my opinion. That's why yours are so good."

Others in the room expressed the same opinion. Phyllis asked for discussion, and it was decided that each lady would be responsible for five cakes each. They'd each bake one and get donations for four more, in order to have a good variety to sell. Oleta brought out the fact that many women didn't enjoy baking but would be eager to have a variety of cakes on the table for Christmas dinner. Cake suggestions included Chocolate, Coconut, Red Velvet, Caramel, Lemon Cheese, Butternut, Lane, and of course, the twins' fruit cake. Phyllis was assigned to bring five Lemon Cheesecakes, Oleta would have five chocolate layer cakes, Frannie would be responsible for the five Coconut Cakes, Daisy said she'd bring five Caramel, and her sister could bring the five fruit cakes, Lula volunteered to bring five Butternut Cakes. Lula said, "It's not like Granny not to show up. I sure hope she's not sick. But we don't have anyone assigned to bring the Red Velvet. Why don't we put her name down to bring five Red Velvet Cakes. You all remember the delicious Red Velvet cake she made for the church Christmas dinner last year."

Everyone was in agreement when the doorbell rang.

Phyllis went to the door and the ladies heard her say. "Granny, we decided you weren't coming."

"Sorry I'm late, but I was waiting for the cake to cool. She walked into the dining room holding a platter of fruit cake slices."

"Oh, but you shouldn't have brought dessert. It's sweet of you, but please take it back home. We've already served refreshments."

"But I want you all to taste it and give me your honest opinion. It's my mama's original fruit cake recipe." She laughed out loud. "There are fruit cakes, and then there are fruit cakes, but I'll guarantee you that none of you have ever tasted one like Mama's, God bless her soul. The secret is getting it to hold together with all the fruit that it calls for."

Oleta said, "But Granny, you came a little late, and Phyllis has already served a beautiful dessert plate. I can't speak for the other ladies, but frankly, I couldn't eat another bite."

Granny smiled. "Phooey! I insist. I went to a lot of trouble to get here. Now—I've got it all figured out, ladies. I got twelve slices out of this one cake. For the festival, we'll slice all the cakes and sell each slice for a dollar. That's very reasonable for the amount of candied fruit that goes into this. Isn't it beautiful? Each piece reminds me of a stained glass window with all the colorful fruit."

Phyllis said, "Granny, it's beautiful, for sure. I'm terribly sorry that you missed the business part of the meeting, but we've decided to have a variety of cakes, and we've already passed out the assignments. We'd like for you to be responsible for five Red Velvet Cakes. You don't have to bake them all yourself—unless you choose to, of course. But there'll be ladies in town who will be happy to donate a cake."

"Land sakes, I have no intention of going around town begging for cakes. That's insane. And I certainly have no plans to bake four fruit cakes plus five Red Velvet Cakes. Why, that would be nine cakes I'd have to take there. No way. It's not necessary. We'll have more than enough cakes with twenty-eight fruit cakes."

Frannie shot a glance toward Oleta. "Did she say twenty-eight?"

Granny said, "Yes, I've brought the recipe to hand out. I figure if we all make four cakes each, then slice each cake into twelve pieces, that'll be seven times four, giving us twenty eight cakes. Then twenty-eight times twelve is three-hundred and thirty-eight slices. That's what I meant when I said we won't need any other cakes."

The room was quiet. Finally, Dixie stood. "If no one else is gonna tell her, then I will. Granny, we had a meeting here today. We voted and you missed it. We won't be needing your fruit cake recipe because I plan to bring the fruit cakes. And if you want to be included on this committee, then you'll go along with the majority, and the majority has spoken."

Daisy looked at her sister, then whispered to Oleta. "Do I know that woman? She looks like my twin, but that can't be Dixie. She's never stood up for herself in her life."

All the ladies sat holding their breath. Suddenly Granny smiled. "Dixie, that's the most I've ever heard come out of your mouth. I reckon you put me in my place. So, which icing do you ladies prefer on Red Velvet Cakes: Buttercream or cream cheese?"

All six yelled, "Cream cheese."

She smiled. "Then cream cheese it is." Then looking over the tops of her spectacles, she giggled. "Good choice. I never did understand why mama put so much candied fruit in her cakes. They look festive, but oh my goodness, it's about the worse cake I've ever tasted."

CHAPTER 19

Tuesday night, Ramona grabbed a mitt and took two pecan pies from the oven. She yelled to her husband, who was reading the evening paper. "Ron, are you busy?"

He put down his paper and walked into the kitchen. "No, what do you need?"

"Nothing."

His mouth gaped open. "Ramona why would you ask if I was busy if you didn't need me?"

"I just wanted to talk to you about something."

He sat down at the kitchen table. "I'm all ears. What's on your mind?"

"I called Deuce this afternoon to ask him what time he and Maddie plan to arrive Thursday."

Ronald seemed confused. "She's in Troy. He's in Jinx Bay. You don't expect them to come together, do you?"

Ramona shook her head. "No, but I thought Deuce would've spoken with her on the phone and would have an idea what time she planned to meet him here. After all, she has no folks, so no one will be looking for her to spend Thanksgiving with them."

"So, what did he say?"

"He said she's not coming. Don't you think that's a bit peculiar? You don't think they're having trouble, do you?"

Ronald chuckled. "I declare, Ramona, when you can't think of something to worry about, you invent something. I'm sure they're fine."

"You're probably right."

"There's something else on your mind. What is it?"

Ramona told him of her suspicions that Peggy might be falling for Joel, but that Joel didn't seem to have a clue. She went on and on for about fifteen minutes, sharing every tiny detail that made her suspect Peggy would be open to a relationship, if only Joel would pursue it.

Ronald reached across the table and took her by the hand. "Stay out of it, sweetheart. It's not like you have to get them together. They're together eight hours a day, five days a week. If there are sparks there, they can start their own flame. They don't need outside influences. Besides, it's not as if they haven't tried it before. It failed."

"But that was different. Joel is not the same man he was back then."

"You're right. But Peggy isn't the same woman, either."

"I don't know why you'd say that."

"Because it's true. She's a mother, now. I'm warning you, Ramona. Don't try to play Cupid. If that's all you wanted to talk about, we can end this conversation, and I'll get back to my crossword puzzle."

Ramona chopped up onions and celery and mixed in with the cornmeal batter. She poured it into a large iron skillet and placed in the oven to bake. Thursday morning, she'd break it up and use it to make the cornbread dressing. She made it by the same recipe she always used, but it was going to be far too much dressing for the four of them. Maybe she should invite Peggy and Joel. She hurried into the living room to mention the idea to her husband.

"Honey, I've just had a terrific idea. It's difficult to cook a large meal for only four people. Why don't we invite Peggy and Joel?"

He laughed. "You don't give up, do you?"

"Well, it makes sense. Neither of them have family here, and besides, the more the merrier, don't you think? They've both already committed to come to our Christmas Dinner. Why not Thanksgiving?"

"Sheesh, Ramona. Why don't you go ahead and make plans for them for Valentine's Day and Fourth of July?"

"You're being facetious. I'm just saying it wouldn't hurt to ask."

"I suppose you're right."

"Good. You call Joel and invite him, then I'll call Peggy." She reached in her apron pocket and smiled. "I just happen to have his number written on a piece of note paper."

Ronald sucked in a lungful of air, then reached over on the end table and picked up the telephone receiver. He looked at the number, then dialed.

Joel answered on the third ring and for the first several minutes, Ronald made small talk about old times and how they needed to set a day aside to go fishing again, like in the good ol' days. Ramona stood beside him nudging him to hurry and invite him. Ronald nodded, indicating that he was getting around to it. "Joel, Ramona, and I would be pleased if you'd honor us by having Thanksgiving Dinner with us on Thursday. Deuce and his girlfriend will be here. You know how my wife likes to cook, and there'll be far too much for the four of us."

Ramona stood waiting. Ronald wasn't saying anything. Finally, he said. "Sure. I understand. Well, good for you. I'm sure you'll enjoy it."

Ramona whispered, "Enjoy what? He's coming, isn't he?"

Ronald made a face at his wife, and she backed off.

He said, "No, Joel, I'm afraid I haven't had the pleasure. A client? Oh! Mr. Grady is the client. Yes I know him. You say she's his daughter? I do remember him mentioning that he had a daughter who was moving back and would be living in the house with him. Well, yes, I suppose that will be different for them both. Sure, I'll tell Ramona. You're welcome. Well, have a good night."

As soon as he hung up the phone, Ramona said, "What was

that all about? He's coming, isn't he?"

"No, he's had a previous invitation."

"From Peggy?"

"No, it seems Peggy has fixed him up with someone else. See, honey. She's not interested, or she wouldn't be trying to set him up with another female."

Ramona found it hard to believe. She was sure she sensed an interest there when she talked with Peggy. But after Ronald told her the whole story, she realized that she'd misinterpreted the signs. "I was so sure she was interested, and I had hoped Joel would return her affections. But if she's the one who set him up, and he accepted, then I'll take your advice and forget about it."

Ronald laughed as if he might be having a hard time believing it.

Ramona checked on the bread, then hurried upstairs and made a phone call from her bedroom.

When Peggy answered, Ramona asked about little Joey, since the last time they spoke Peggy had commented that he was ill from cutting teeth. Then she got around to the purpose for her call. Trying to sound nonchalant, she mentioned Ronald just happened to talk to Joel and that Joel just happened to mention that he'd be having Thanksgiving Dinner with a woman who'd been in the office a few times, whose father was a client of his. Then, she waited, hoping for an explanation.

Peggy said, "That's right. Her name is Darla Grady. She's a beautiful woman. I encouraged Joel to call and invite her out for

Thanksgiving Dinner. Andy's Steakhouse will be open, and they plan to serve a traditional Thanksgiving Meal." She went on to explain that when Joel called the woman, Darla asked him to allow her the privilege of preparing dinner for him. Peggy said, "I think they'll be perfect for one another. She's beautiful, and smart . . . and available. And he's handsome, and smart and sweet, and he's . . . I'm sorry, Ramona. I think I hear the baby crying."

Ramona said, "Peggy, I don't think that's the baby. You're crying, aren't you? What's wrong?"

"I'm crying because I'm so stupid."

"Then I was right. You are in love with Joel aren't you? You are! So, why would you set him up with someone else?"

Peggy admitted it was a crazy idea, but she wanted to find out if he had feelings for her. She thought she'd insist he call Darla and ask her out, but deep down she was hoping he'd refuse. When he didn't, it shattered her hopes.

Ramona wanted to console her, but she couldn't find the words to say. Perhaps something would come to her later. She invited her and little Joey to be at Rose Trellis at noon on Thursday to share a meal with the family.

CHAPTER 20

Tuesday evening Candy met Marti at the Jinx Bay First Community Church to practice the Children's Christmas Pageant. The children were all excited and had practiced their parts. As the Christmas story unfolded before her eyes, Candy jumped up and ran out. Stunned, yet attempting to hide her concern, Marti said, "Kids, how many of you know how to pray?"

Every little hand shot up in the air. Jason said, "I will, Miss Thompson. Let me, please!"

"I need you all to pray, while I go talk to Miss Candy. I'd like you all to pray silently until I return."

Holly said, "What are we praying for?"

Jenna, who always seemed to have the answers, said, "Don't you know? Miss Candy has a problem:"

Marti ran out the door, searching for her friend. Car lights came on, and Candy was backing out of the parking lot, when

Marti ran to stop her.

Candy stopped. "I can't do this Marti. I'm sorry. I can't. I've got to go."

"Hold on, Candy. Talk to me. What happened?"

"I'm not sure. I just know I can't do this."

Marti looked at her watch. "It's time for the kids' parents to come pick them up. Let me go back inside. But please don't leave. Not until we have a chance to talk." She hurried back inside and smiled seeing all the children on their knees, praying. All except Bradley, who was quietly flying paper airplanes he'd made from church bulletins he found in the backs of pews. Marti smiled. Seeing the children praying was heartwarming, but the fact that Bradley had quietly found something to do was a miracle. She wanted to hug them all. "Amen!" She announced. "Thank you all for all your prayers."

A nine-year-old with pigtails said, "Did God fix Miss Candy's problem, yet?"

"If not already, he will soon, sweetheart, for I know he heard every prayer. Now, let's go stand under the shelter and wait for your parents." She looked across the parking lot and was glad to see the red convertible sitting in the same place she left it.

After the last child was picked up, she hurried over to Candy's car, opened the door and slid in. "We need to talk. Follow me to my house."

"Why? It won't change things. I need to leave. I never should've agreed to do this."

"Candy, I've known from the first night we met at the Council meeting that God brought you into my life for a reason."

Candy's eyes squinted. "If you only knew my story, you wouldn't say that."

"Your story? Don't you realize we all have a story?"

She laid her head on the steering wheel and sobbed. "Not like mine."

Marti threw her arms around her neck, before getting out. "I'll see you at the apartment."

She walked over to an old rusted out Studebaker, and got in. Candy waited for her to pull away, but the car went dead three or four times before the engine revved and the old car chugged away.

Candy was surprised when Marti turned down a road in dire need of repaving and wound up at a low-rent housing complex. *This is it? This is where she lives?.* Never would she have expected to find Marti Thompson living in such a heap. She was so . . . so put together. But more than that, she seemed so content. Not only content, but happy. How could that be possible? Candy thought about what she had said, "Everybody has a story." Now, she was more anxious than ever to hear hers.

When Marti invited her in, Candy was surprised to see such a neat, cozy little room. Marti led her into the tiny kitchen and offered her a seat at a little table for two, while she put on a pot of coffee.

Marti reached in the cabinet and took out a couple of Moon

Pies from a box. Smiling, she tossed one to Candy. "I love these things. I hope you do, too. I'm not much of a baker, so it's all I have to offer you."

Candy unwrapped the giant cookie. "This is great. Thanks."

"Marti, why did you say you think God put me in your life for a reason? Is it because of the kind of car I drive, or the clothes I wear? Did you look at me and think I might have the means to help you, financially?"

Marti squinted. "I don't think I understand what you're asking."

"I'm sorry. That didn't come out right. I mean no disrespect, but I have a feeling you could use some help. Please don't be embarrassed. I've been in situations before where I could appreciate someone offering to help pull me out of a jam."

Marti smiled. "Oh, my precious friend. You are so sweet to want to help, and I thank you. But I'm fairing just fine. The Lord is my Shepherd, I shall not want. I suppose you looked around the neighborhood and felt sorry for me, but please don't. I am exactly where God has planted me for this chapter of my life. But I didn't invite you here to talk about me. Who are *you*, Candy McCoy?"

Candy fidgeted with the emerald ring on her finger. "Not much to know. I'm from Tampa, my daddy owns a couple of banks, my mother is into pharmaceuticals and stays busy with several charities. I graduated from Secretarial School in Montgomery, and after working for a bank there, I left to be near the beach. That's it in a nutshell. Not much to tell." She pushed her coffee aside. "I really should go."

Marti reached for her hand. "What's troubling you, Candy?"

She feigned a laugh. "I don't know what you mean?"

"I think you do. Whatever you're going through, I want you to know I'm here for you."

"That's because you don't know me."

"You just told me who you are."

With her elbows on the table and her face hid in her hands, Candy sobbed. "I lied to you. Just like I've lied to everyone else. If you knew the truth, you wouldn't walk on the same side of the street with me."

Marti squeezed her hand. "Is that what the devil has been telling you?"

"What?"

"God says you are wonderfully and fearfully made. That he loves you so much that he sent his Son to pay for your sins by going to the cross, so you wouldn't owe for them. But that's not what the devil wants you to hear. He wants to tell you that you're worthless. You're listening to the wrong voice if that's what you're hearing."

"But it's true. I'm not like you. You're good."

"No, Candy. I'm not good. But I'm Redeemed. It's Christ in me that's good."

Candy stared into Marti's eyes. "You asked me to tell you who I am. Well, here goes, and I'll go ahead and turn in my resignation on the Pageant Committee, so you won't have to tell me to leave. This is who I am: My name is Candy McCoy. That part that you know about me is true. It's the only part that's true. When I said my daddy owns a couple of banks, I wasn't referring to my biological father. I have no idea who he might be. I was referring to my 'sugar daddy.'"

Marti swallowed hard. "I don't understand."

"Of course, you don't. I didn't expect you to. I grew up dirt poor. I told you Mama was into pharmaceuticals. In other words, she was a dope peddler. I also said she was involved in various charities. True. She went from one charity to another, taking whatever they had to hand out.

While I was at Massey Draughn, I worked parttime at a bank. The owner of the bank took a liking to me, and I soon figured out that he was my ticket out of the slums."

"But you were going to school, preparing yourself for a brighter future. Didn't you feel that was your ticket?"

"That's what I told myself when I enrolled in school, but when Jack—that was his name—began offering to take me back to the YWCO where I lived, it seemed innocent at first. The bank was on Dexter and the 'Y' was on St. Lawrence Street. Not too far to walk, but I figured why not ride when the opportunity was there. Then he began thinking of reasons why I should stay late after closing. The first time he kissed me, it took me by surprise. Me, a nobody, and here's this rich man who's interested in someone like me?

Although he was old enough to be my father, I found him

attractive. He's tall, has a great build, and the silver hair at his temples compliments his deep tan. All the women in the bank were always making remarks about working for such a hunk. And I'm thinking, of all the beautiful women he could have, he chooses me?"

"I guess you were flattered."

"Of course I was flattered. It wasn't long before the rides home began to include dinners at remote locations. Never in Montgomery. He said the bank owned a beautiful penthouse in a high-rise hotel one street over from the bank, and offered to let me stay there. I told him I was sure I couldn't afford it, but he said not to worry. It was taken care of."

"What did you think?"

"Truthfully? Or are you asking what I should've thought? Because truthfully, I wasn't so naïve that I didn't know why he was being so generous, nor what his expectations were. But for a country girl who grew up without indoor plumbing, I began to picture myself married to a rich, handsome man who treated me like a queen. I think I knew deep down that he had no plans to marry me, although he pretended that to be his intention. But I was confident enough in my looks to believe I could eventually change his mind. He gave me a credit card to Blumberg's and gave me my car."

"Was he married?"

"Divorced."

"I assume the relationship ended, since you left and came

132

here."

"Yeah."

Marti didn't know whether to ask the question preying on her mind, or whether to allow Candy to tell only what she was comfortable revealing.

Candy smiled. "I see I've left you speechless. I warned you that I was worthless. I guess you'll believe me now. If you'd like to get my coat for me, I'll leave and won't be bothering you again."

"Girlfriend, I won't let you off the hook that easily. You promised to help me with the Christmas Pageant, and I plan to hold you to it."

Her brow scrunched together. "Are you serious? You still want me to work with you? At the church?"

"Why wouldn't I?"

Candy's chin trembled. "I've never had a friend like you." Then with a quirky grin, she added, "And I suppose you've never had one like me."

Her comment made Marti laugh. "No, you and I are both one-of-a-kind. That's for sure."

CHAPTER 21

Troy, Alabama
Wednesday, November 24th

Maddie turned over in the bed and looked at the clock radio at five-forty-five, Wednesday morning. After tossing and turning all night, unable to sleep, she saw no reason to believe sleep would come now. She sat up and put her feet on the floor.

Grabbing her robe, she ambled into the kitchen, took a quart of milk from the fridge, and sat down at the table with a bowl of cereal. But after taking the first bite, she shoved the bowl aside. If she tried to swallow another spoonful, she'd choke.

If only she hadn't been so eager. That had always been her problem. No patience. Why had she felt that mailing the letter was so urgent that she couldn't have waited a couple of days to see if she'd get the job? Now, it looked as if she had lost Deuce and the job. Maddie was scared.

She'd been frightened before, but this was a new kind of fear.

It wasn't like when she feared for her life while being held captive at the Habersham House. Nothing could ever be that frightening. She shuddered recalling Victor and the threats that were made on her life. Though she was in no danger at the present of being physically violated, the fear that she was about to lose everything that meant something to her prevented her from eating, sleeping, or being able to think straight. What made it especially hard was knowing that she had brought the current trauma on herself.

She walked over and turned on the television, then went and laid down on the sofa. Captain Kangaroo was on, but since it was the only channel she could get, she didn't bother to get up to turn it off. Besides, she was rather fond of Mr. Green Jeans. When the picture on the set began to flicker on and off, she got off the sofa, walked over and tried to adjust the antennae. When she couldn't get a clear picture, she turned off the set and walked back into the kitchen.

She had just placed her cereal bowl in the sink, when the phone rang. It was Coach Weeks, apologizing for her failure to keep the interview.

Maddie's heart thumped so hard it felt as if it would leap out of her chest. She braced herself for the bad news, knowing if it had been good, the coach would've called sooner. Until now, she had blamed the coach for not having the guts to call and tell her in person. Her feelings had changed in the last two minutes. Why couldn't the woman have sent a letter instead of putting her in the awkward position of trying to be a gracious loser?

Coach Weeks said, "Maddie, we are just beginning to formally participate in intercollegiate competitions at Auburn and we're seeking the most qualified candidates to lead our program. Your name has been offered and it would give me great pleasure to interview you for that position."

Maddie's throat tightened. She tried to swallow, but there wasn't enough saliva to cause the knot to go down.

"We've finished most of the interviews and have narrowed the prospects down to two."

Maddie placed her hand over her mouth. Was the coach saying what she thought she was saying?

She asked Maddie to meet her at her office at nine o'clock sharp, on December 3rd, a week from Friday.

As soon as she hung up the phone, she fell back on the sofa. Why did she have to wait a whole week? But Maddie was too excited to allow herself to question the timing. She was still in the running. Didn't the coach say there were only two left? She went over the entire conversation in her mind. That's exactly what she said. Two!

Maddie was almost glad Coach Weeks missed the previous appointment. She wasn't at all happy with the dress she'd worn the day of the original interview. The drab color faded her out and the gathered skirt made her hips look wide. She needed to wear something bright—something that would make her appear healthy, as well as something that would show off her toned figure. Something clingy, but not too clingy.

But when would she have time to shop? Her Troy basketball team would be participating in a Charity tournament all next week, and she'd have very little time to look for something appropriate to wear on the interview. If only she hadn't promised her six-year-old niece she could spend Thanksgiving with her, she could spend all day today and tomorrow shopping for the perfect attire. It was a bad time to be baby-sitting, but she couldn't back out on the kid at such a late date. Tina would never forgive her if she left her at the Children's Home on Thanksgiving.

She glanced at her watch. It was eight-thirty, and the stores had advertised a nine-o'clock opening for Wednesday morning with two days of huge Holiday sales. It wouldn't be as much time as she'd like to have, but if she got downtown as soon as the stores opened, and waited until mid-afternoon to pick up Tina, it should give her plenty of time to try on everything in her two favorite stores.

Picking up the phone, she called the Children's Home and told them something had come up that would prevent her from coming for Tina at ten o'clock, as previously planned. She'd be there at three that afternoon.

The substitute housemother told her how excited Tina had been, and how the home was practically empty. Even the children who didn't have family had been picked up by foster families willing to give a child a special Thanksgiving. "Your precious little niece will be heartbroken that she'll have to wait here until mid-afternoon, with all her friends gone, but I suppose you have to do what you have to do. I'm just saying she's gonna be a sad little girl."

Maddie could see the woman was trying to put a guilt trip on her for not picking Tina up sooner. If the truth were known, the old bag probably wanted to get rid of her so she wouldn't have to put up with her.

Maddie would've gladly picked her up, if it hadn't been for the fact that her time was limited, and the interview was the most important thing that had ever happened to her. Finding the perfect outfit would take time. With a pencil and note pad, she decided to write down what the perfect outfit would look like. It had to be sporty but not masculine. Yet she didn't want to look so "girly" that it could give the impression that she couldn't be taken seriously as a basketball coach.

She closed her eyes trying to picture such a dress. No doubt about it, it wouldn't be easy to walk in a store and pull it off a rack. She shopped every store in Troy, trying on everything that came close to what she had in mind. At twelve-fifteen, discouraged, she decided there was nothing that came close to what she was looking for. That's when she decided if she hurried, she could get to Normandale Shopping Center in Montgomery and be back by three o'clock. The selection would be much better there.

The time flew by, but she finally found exactly what she was looking for: A fitted corduroy skirt with a bright orange sweater. She was so tired of wearing summer clothes, it had been fun searching through all the new fall and winter fashions. She tried it on, and decided it was worth every minute she spent searching for it.

She paid for it, then hurried out to the car. She looked at her watch. *Four-thirty?* Impossible. By the time she reached Troy, it was getting dark. Maddie hurried into the Home and was met by glaring eyes. The substitute housemother snarled, "Shame on you! Tina has had enough adults to disappoint her. You didn't need to add your name to the list."

"I don't know what you're talking about. I'm here to take her home with me to spend the night so we can spend Thanksgiving together, tomorrow. Please ring for her."

The gripey old woman looked behind her and pointed to a giant clock on the wall. "Do you see the time? You promised her you'd be here at three o'clock."

Offended at being reprimanded, Maddie shot back. "I made no promises. I said I'd try. And I did try, but something came up."

"More important than the child's faith in you?"

Maddie rolled her eyes. "Where is she?"

"In her room, crying her eyes out. She decided you weren't coming, and frankly I thought she was probably right."

"Well, you weren't right. I'm here, and I'd appreciate it if you'd let her know."

"You're welcome to go to her room and make sure she has all she needs to stay overnight. That is, unless you decide to bring her back tonight."

Maddie felt badly enough. She didn't need this woman

rubbing salt into her wounds. She rushed up the stairs to Tina's room. She was all alone, and just as the woman predicted, Tina was lying across her bed, sobbing.

Maddie walked over and sat down beside her. "Hey, why the tears?"

She turned over and wiped her eyes. "I thought you weren't coming."

"I told you I'd be here, didn't I?"

"But you said three o'clock."

"I did, and I'm sorry. I'll make it up to you." Maddie packed an overnight bag for Tina, then took her out for a hamburger and ice cream, before going to the apartment.

It wasn't long before all was forgiven, and Tina was saying Maddie was her favorite aunt—which would've been gratifying if not for the fact she was Tina's only aunt.

CHAPTER 22

This Thanksgiving Day was certainly going to be different from the way Deuce had anticipated. The thought that Maddie might break up with him and that he'd be traveling to have dinner with his parents alone, had never entered his mind. He had trusted her. He was so sure that she felt as strongly toward him as he did toward her. Apparently, he was fooled.

He recalled the last time she drove to Jinx Bay. It was only five, maybe six weeks ago. They were so happy. Or at least that's what he thought at the time. They made sandwiches, brewed a jug of sweet tea, threw in a couple of apples and a bag of cookies, and picnicked on the pier.

They pulled off their shoes and walked along the edge of the water. She rolled up her pants legs and tied her shirt in a knot, with her midriff showing. He knew she had a great figure, but he hadn't realized what great shape she was in, until he saw more of her that day than he'd ever seen before.

As they walked along the edge of the bay, they talked about how wonderful it would be when they could be together forever. He hadn't realized how short forever would be.

Before she left to go back home to her job, they made plans to meet at his parents' estate, Rose Trellis in Eufaula, at ten o'clock, November 25th. Thanksgiving morning. She'd be traveling from Troy, and he'd be leaving from Jinx Bay.

He told her how excited his mother was when he told her they'd be there, and Maddie remarked how much she had enjoyed having Christmas dinner with the family last year.

His mother loved to cook, and holidays gave her an opportunity to really show out. She loved it, but so did Deuce. It wasn't just about the food, although if that had been all there was to it, it would've been enough. But there was so much more that made it a very special day. It was the joy that permeated throughout the house—the funny stories, the teasing, the laughter, the hugs. And the friends. No one ever knew for sure who might show up, but his mother invariably would find someone she felt wouldn't have family around to share the day with. For that one special day, they'd become a part of the Jones family. It all was as much a part of Thanksgiving as the turkey on the table.

Now, Maddie wouldn't be there, and he'd be left to answer all the haunting questions about what happened between them. How could he explain something he couldn't understand himself? Deuce realized she was athletic and loved playing ball. But couldn't she do that in a high school setting? Was coaching high school girls really any different than coaching college girls? The only difference he could see was that they were a year older. It didn't make sense. If she loved him, she wouldn't have put a career ahead of him.

The truth was being revealed. She didn't love him. The letter was proof. Sure, he would've preferred having her stay home, and raise the kids he hoped to have, but not once had he even suggested that to her.

If she had her heart set on coaching—and she did—then he had no plans to ask her to give up something she really loved. They could've married as planned and she could've coached at a local school the way they talked about when they first discussed marriage. What happened to that idea?

She told him that she had sent her resume to schools in Okaloosa County. He wasn't sure how many responses she had received, but all she needed was one, and he knew for a fact she had heard from at least two.

Deuce's heart was full, and his throat ached when he tried to swallow. The past memories, which previously filled him with hope and brought comfort on lonely nights, now felt more like a recurring nightmare.

If only she'd tell him what he did wrong. Was it something he said that caused her to stop loving him? He thought back to the night when they first met. What was it about her that stole his breath and made his stomach tie in knots at the very sight of her? No female had had such an effect on him since his sweet Margo.

He bristled, angry at himself for even comparing the two. Maddie and Margo weren't even in the same category.

He fell in love with Margo when he was only fifteen years old. Some tried to say it was "puppy love—kid stuff." But they were wrong. It was real. More real than anything he'd ever known or could ever hope to know. The day they laid her in the ground, he made himself a promise that he'd never allow another girl to take her place. How could he? She was one of a kind. Deuce attempted to swallow the lump growing in his throat. He looked at his watch. He'd promised his mother he wouldn't be late for dinner, but he had plenty of time.

Before leaving town, he drove down Cannery Road, and stopped at Cabin #5, the little shanty where Margo had lived with her fisherman father. Juan Lopez.

The doctors claimed Mr. Lopez had congestive heart failure, but Deuce knew what was really wrong with him. It was heart failure, alright—not from too much fluid, but too much loneliness. Margo was Mr. Lopez's heart, and the day she died, the life drained from her doting father. He was no longer physically able to work, but because of his long service with the company, he was allowed to continue living in the cabin he'd occupied for years.

Deuce sat in the car, staring at the little porch as the precious, yet heart-wrenching memories flooded his thoughts. He got out, walked up the crude steps and knocked on the door. Not waiting for an answer, he stuck his head inside and called out: "Mr. Lopez, it's Deuce."

His heart sank, seeing a skeletal of a man slumped over in a worn easy chair. Was he dead? How long had he been there? He walked over and picked up his wrist.

The old man opened his eyes. "Deuce? Deuce, my boy. So good to see you."

Deuce's heart hammered. "Good to see you, too, Mr. Lopez."

The old man's face brightened, and it was evident he appreciated the visit. Deuce was ashamed that his visits had become sparse, but he made a promise to himself that he'd be more attentive in the future.

Mr. Lopez was interested in everything taking place in Deuce's life. He asked about the fishermen, especially the older ones who fished with him for years. He wanted to know about the Cannery, and they talked about Margo, and both broke down and shed a few tears. Then, Mr. Lopez said, "You've told me everything I want to know, except how you're doing."

He feigned a smile. "Me? I'm great. I love being back in Jinx Bay."

"But what about love?"

Deuce frowned. "It was great. I'll always love Margo."

"But Margo is gone and you're a young man with a life ahead of you. Son, I know my Margo and I know if she could look down from Heaven with advice for you, she'd say, 'Love again, Deuce. Find love again.'"

Deuce's Adam's apple bobbed when he swallowed. "I tried, sir. It'll never be the same as with Margo."

"It doesn't need to be the same. My beautiful daughter was your first love. There'll never be another first love, but it doesn't mean there can't be another kind of love. One just as precious, just as real. Find her. For Margo. Find her."

Deuce sucked in a deep breath. "I thought I had."

"But—?"

"We didn't want the same things."

"Couldn't you reach a compromise?"

"No sir."

"Then I won't pry." When Mr. Lopez began to cough, he pointed to a cabinet. "Would you mind getting the cough syrup and a spoon?"

"Water?"

"No, I don't drink water afterward."

Deuce gave him the medicine. Noting that the more Mr. Lopez talked, the worse the cough became, he said his goodbyes and left, with a promise to return soon. He also made a promise to himself. As soon as he got back after the holidays, he'd buy Margo's daddy a brand-new reclining leather easy chair. One that could swivel toward the door or the TV, since he'd noticed how difficult it was for him to shift his worn-out body.

So many unanswered questions swirled around in Deuce's head as he drove from Jinx Bay to Eufaula to attend his mother's annual Thanksgiving Dinner. His least favorite foods in all the world happened to be turkey, cranberry sauce, and cornbread dressing, the three main staples that appeared on the table every Thanksgiving. If only the Pilgrims had decided to have barbecue ribs and corn on the cob, he would've been much happier.

With his mind so full of other things, he didn't remember going through Bruce on the way home, or he would've at least stopped for a cup of coffee.

His mind had not been on the road, but on his stupidity for being taken for a sucker.

CHAPTER 23

Thanksgiving morning, Ramona made out a timesheet to make sure all the food would come out of the oven at a proper time to have it all hot and on the table by twelve noon. At six o'clock that morning, as she cooked breakfast, she put on a fresh hen to boil, to use in her dressing.

After breakfast she turned on the oven and waited for it to reach the desired temperature to bake her dressing. She baked it exactly the way she'd done for years, but when she took it from the oven, it was so badly burned, it stuck to the bottom of the pan.

Ronald, knowing how upset she was, assured her that dressing was not his nor Deuce's favorite dish. He said, "As long as you have your famous sweet potato casserole, we wouldn't care if there was nothing else on the table."

Still, Ramona fretted, thinking it wouldn't seem like Thanksgiving without the dressing. She took the turkey out of the refrigerator, made a tent around it with tinfoil and slid it into the oven. The aroma soon filled the room. It was a beautiful bird, and much larger than the four of them could eat, but she knew how much Ronald loved turkey sandwiches. There'd be plenty for sandwiches and she'd send some of the meat home with Peggy.

Peggy arrived at eleven o'clock and Deuce drove up only minutes afterward. Ramona invited them to have a seat in the parlor. When Peggy offered to help, Ramona assured her everything was taken care of. "The turkey is roasting in the top oven, and I have the sweet potato casserole baking in the bottom oven. I put the turkey in first and timed it so both should be ready at the same time."

She was dying to ask Deuce why Maddie decided not to come, but Ronald had warned her not to pry and said that if he wanted them to know, he'd tell them. She'd secretly felt it would be good to have her son all to herself. But now, she wasn't so sure. He was acting moody, which wasn't like Deuce at all. Something was wrong and she knew it. He had very little to say and spent his time playing with Joey.

"Deuce, will Maddie's little niece be staying at the Children's Home, or will she have an opportunity to spend the day with Maddie?"

He lifted a shoulder in a shrug. "Dunno."

"I suppose that's why she decided not to come. Maybe she plans to do something special with the child. Do you think maybe that might be the reason she cancelled?"

Ronald, anticipating where the conversation was headed, said, "Son, come outside with me. I'd like to show you something. We'll take Joey with us. I'm sure he'd like to feel the cool air on his little face."

Ramona's muscles tightened. She knew exactly what her husband was doing. If he wanted her to stop with the questions, why didn't he just say so?

Then seeing a worried look on Peggy's face, she said, "Tell me if it's none of my business, Peg, but I've got a gut feeling that you're troubled about something. Can I help?"

Wearing a fake smile, she said, "It must be your imagination, Ramona. Everything is great. It's a lovely day, and I'm so grateful you invited Joey and me to join you for this beautiful occasion. I've been looking forward to it."

"I wish Joel could've joined us. I enjoyed having him here last Christmas. But tell me about the woman you fixed him up with. Do you think something might come of it?"

"Who knows? Maybe. His plan was to take her out to dinner, but she told me she planned to cook a turkey dinner for him, instead. I'm sure she's a great cook. She can do everything else."

Ramona wasn't sure, but she thought she heard a hint of sarcasm in Peggy's voice.

When the stove timer went off, Ramona opened the back door and called the guys in to eat. "Time to wash up. The turkey and casserole are ready to come out of the ovens."

She opened a drawer and took out two mitts. Then opening the top oven, she shrieked.

Ronald ran into the kitchen. "What's going on? Don't tell me the turkey burned, too." His eyes widened when she pulled out the roasting pan. "Good grief! What happened? Did you forget to turn the stove back on?"

"No." She pointed to the temperature knob. "You can see for yourself. It's still set, but this turkey is raw."

He put his arm around her. "I suppose the element burned out. Don't worry about it, hon."

"How can you say not to worry? We have nothing to eat and it's Thanksgiving. I am so embarrassed."

Peggy overheard the conversation. "Hey, I'm sorry that it happened to you, Ramona. I know you spent a lot of time with the preparation, but we won't let it spoil our day. Why don't we go to Andy's Steakhouse for lunch? The menu in the paper sounded terrific."

Trying to hold in the tears, Ramona said, "Are you sure?"

Deuce chuckled. "Mom, if she's as hungry as I am, then I'll guarantee you that she's sure. Let's go!"

Ronald said, "We can all ride in the station wagon."

CHAPTER 24

Joel went by to pick up Darla—more as a favor to Peggy than by choice. He supposed Peggy felt sorry for the woman, since Darla appeared to spend all of her time either working or taking care of business for her cantankerous, elderly father.

He couldn't imagine that Peggy's life could be much different, since her days were consumed with either work or caring for Joey. But Joel concluded that taking care of a sweet baby who needed her was much different than someone who sought to meet the needs of an ornery old codger like Mr. Grady. And that was being gentle. The old fellow was a pain to deal with in the office. Joel could only imagine what Darla went through, living with him.

He reached in the seat and picked up the wrist corsage he ordered from the florist. It had been too long since he had dated, and he didn't know what was proper anymore. He'd gone back and forth over whether he should bring flowers, and if so, what kind or how many. He finally settled on a wrist corsage. He recalled giving his date one for the Prom, but that was over twenty years ago. What if the corsage sent a message that he was interested in having a relationship? That was the last thing in the world he wanted or needed at this point in his life. He opened the glove compartment and stuffed the corsage inside, before getting out of the car.

He knocked on the door, and Mr. Grady answered. Mr. Grady looked him over. "Lawyer Gunter! What are you doing here?"

Before he could answer, Darla walked in looking lovelier than Joel remembered ever seeing her. He shifted on his feet and said, "You look really, really good." He winced at repeating 'really,' although she really did. "What I mean is you look very beautiful."

Mr. Grady rolled his eyes. "Don't you mean, very, very beautiful?" He stepped between his daughter and Joel. "I asked you a question. What are you doing here?" Then the old codger turned and stared at his daughter. "Darla go get you on some clothes. That dress is so low I thought it was a skirt at first."

Joel was embarrassed for her, but it didn't seem to faze her. "I have on clothes, Daddy, and Joel is here to pick me up. I'm sure I told you he was coming to take me to dinner. I'll bring you home a plate."

"He's here to pick you up? Is that what you've come to? Dating divorced men? Don't misunderstand, Joel, I like you fine for a lawyer, but I'm not too keen on you dating my daughter. I have ears. I've heard that you've been around the block a time or two. She's never been married, you know. I'd hate to think you might take advantage of my little girl."

"I understand, Mr. Grady."

"Good. Because if I should ever hear of you putting your hands on her, I'll personally hunt you down. So, be warned. If you have any thoughts of such, I'd advise you to make sure your hospital insurance is current."

Darla shrieked. "Daddy, that was uncalled for. Please apologize."

"I apologize when I'm wrong. I meant every word I said."

Joel said, "I understand, sir, and I promise to treat her as if she's my sister."

She apologized all the way to the car, but he assured her that her father had every right to want to protect her. Joel had never paid much attention to her looks, but now that he was looking her over, Peggy was right. Darla Grady was a good-looking woman. It made him wonder how she'd managed to stay single so long. A man would be crazy for not wanting to go out with someone with her looks and brains.

So, he was crazy! But he'd already used up his quota for messing up lives. The last thing the woman needed would be to fall for a guy like him. Besides, she was off limits for two good reasons: (1) He wouldn't put it past Mr. Grady to swear out a warrant on him if he so much as kissed her goodnight, and (2) he'd already sworn off serious relationships.

However, the only reason he agreed to set up this date was to stop Peggy from nagging him to spend Thanksgiving Day with Darla. The day he approached Darla and asked her out, she had offered to prepare a home-cooked meal for him, instead. It scared the begeezies out of him. No way would he fall into that trap! He was too smart to let a woman start fussing over him by talking him into playing house with her. The next thing would be her wanting to sit him down in a comfy chair in her parlor and take him a pair of slippers and a cigar. No sir buddy, he was too smart for that.

That wouldn't appeal to him even if her old man hadn't given him an ultimatum. He was insistent that they go out to eat.

Peggy had said Andy planned to keep the Steakhouse open for Thanksgiving and would have the traditional Holiday meal. However, Joel preferred steak over turkey, so it was a perfect place to go.

He was surprised at how much he enjoyed Darla's company. Her quick wit kept him laughing. It was good to laugh. It had been a new experience for him lately, and he was loving it.

****

The restaurant was crowded. Ramona was surprised to find so many people who would have chosen to go out instead of having a nice dinner at home. The waitress told them it was buffet style and to help themselves. Peggy sat Joey in a highchair at the table, then followed the others to the buffet table.

She turned around when someone in line tapped her on the shoulder. She swallowed hard. "Darla! I thought you . . . you and Joel—"

Darla said, "You thought we'd be eating at my house? I

volunteered but Joel insisted we come to Andy's. If you're here alone, you're welcome to come sit at our table."

"Thanks, but I'm with friends." She glanced back of Darla. Her gaze locked with Joel's. He gave a slight nod of his head, and in a muffled tone, he said something that she interpreted to be, "Hi, Peggy, or How are ya, Peg." She couldn't make it out, but she returned the nod and mumbled, "Fine," hoping it was the correct response.

Suddenly she was not hungry, but she put a small slice of turkey on her plate and a tiny helping of green bean casserole. She dipped cream potatoes for Joey, then went to sit down.

Ramona, Ronald, and Deuce were already seated, and Deuce had given Joey a roll. She smiled. "I thought he was being unusually quiet. He normally gets a little rambunctious when he smells food. Patience isn't one of his virtues."

Everyone laughed, and she was glad they could find humor in her comment. Her lips felt as if they'd crack when she pretended to laugh with them. All she wanted to do was to go home, put Joey down for a nap and squall.

After lunch, Ronald drove them back to Rose Trellis, and Peggy said she wouldn't go in, since it was past Joey's naptime. When Peggy offered to let her take him into one of the bedrooms to lay him down, she made an excuse. "Thank you, but we really should go. But it was so nice being able to share Thanksgiving with some of my favorite friends."

Deuce sat Joey in his car seat, in the front seat, next to Peggy.

As soon as he walked in the door, his mom said, "Deuce, your dad told me not to meddle, but—"

Ronald said, "But she can't help herself. Ramona, don't pester him."

"I don't intend to pester him, but I am interested in what's going on in his life and I want to know why Maddie chose not to be here with him."

Deuce plopped down in a chair. "Mom, why are you so sure she chose not to be here. Maybe I didn't want her here."

"Because I know you, and I know you love her, so something has to be bad wrong."

"Forget it."

"Honey, I can't forget it. I love you and I don't like to see you hurting. You hardly said a word at lunch."

He rolled his eyes and stood.

"Where are you going?"

"Home."

"What do you mean, home? You *are* home."

He made no comment but walked upstairs to get his bag.

Ronald said, "I warned you not to press him. You know when he wants to talk, he will, but if you push him, he's gonna clam up and you'll never get it out of him."

He came back down minutes later, holding his duffel bag. He walked over and threw his arms around his mother. "I'm sorry things didn't turn out the way you wanted, but sometimes that's how life goes. I love you, Mom, but I need to go."

"Oh, honey, please stay. You said you have the whole weekend off. Why would you want to go back and stay in that old cabin all alone when you could be here with us? We miss you so much."

"I know you don't understand, Mom. But I've gotta do what I've gotta do."

"And what exactly does that mean? It doesn't even make sense."

"Bye Mom." He walked over and held out his hand to shake with his dad, when Ronald grabbed him in a hug. "It was good seeing you, son. Be careful driving back."

He walked away with Ramona crying. He knew she meant no harm. She was truly interested in what was going on in his life. But it still felt too raw to discuss it. If only he knew why Maddie broke up with him. He'd replayed their last conversation over in his head hundreds of times but could think of nothing that would've caused her to write that letter. Was it another guy? That had to be the answer. There was no other logical explanation.

CHAPTER 25

Deuce questioned his motives for leaving home early, and every reason that he came up with led to the same conclusion. He was being downright selfish. It wasn't something he wanted to admit, yet neither was it something he could deny.

When he packed up to leave Eufaula, he had no thoughts for anyone other than himself. He'd had disappointments before, but none had ever led to him having such a pity party. He didn't want to feel this way. It was childish.

He knew his mother was hurt and she had every right to be. She'd looked forward to Thanksgiving since the last one they were together. Family had always been important to her. Maybe she obsessed over the holidays, but could he blame her? She missed so many when his father was out of their lives, and when they were finally reunited, she must've wanted to make up for lost time.

Yet, he hardly spent any time with her while he was home,

and when she tried to talk to him, he cut her off. This day meant a lot to her, yet it all fell apart.

Hadn't she been through enough of a disappointment when the stove failed to work? Why did he have to add to her troubles? Was it necessary for him to strike out for Jinx Bay as early as he did? The answer was no.

Sure, he hated answering a barrage of questions but was it so terrible that he had a mother who was genuinely interested in everything he did? Could he not spare her one day out of his life?

The guilt almost made him get on the truck and head back to Eufaula. Almost. Instead, he wandered around the cabin, searching for something to interest him. He tried to watch the Macy's Thanksgiving Parade on television, but he soon realized his eyes were glued to the set, but his mind was a hundred miles away in Troy, Alabama.

He drove over to the Fish Camp. The eerie quietness gave him chills. He lumbered out to Boggy Bayou, thinking if anything could pull him out of such a depressed feeling, it would be seeing the sun set on the water. It always seemed to brighten his mood.

He tried to get Maddie off his mind, but every thought seemed to lead straight back to her. What had he done to cause her to fall out of love with him? Can one really fall out of love? Or is it a sign they were never in love in the beginning?

Maybe she never really loved him, but if she didn't, she should audition for a part in the movies, because she sure had him fooled. His thoughts carried him back to the night they first met.

He was smitten at first glance. He recalled the alluring way she looked in the kitchen that night, and how he longed to wrap his arms around her. He liked everything about her—her looks, her smile, her laughter, her sweetness, her sense of humor, and the way she made him feel when she looked at him. But was it love? Real love? Or merely a sexual attraction that drew him to a beautiful woman? He couldn't be sure. But if it wasn't real, then what does real love feel like? Weren't all those things the same things he loved about Margo? There was no doubt in his mind that what he felt for her was true love.

There was one thing for sure. He might've been fooled by Maddie, but he'd never be fooled again. His throat tightened when he recalled saying the same thing after he lost Margo.

He sat on the dock with his feet hanging in the cool bay, as he waited to see the sun set on the water—a sight he never tired of seeing. Yet he looked around and realized the sun had gone down while he sat there, and he didn't even see it happening. He had to get a grip.

He walked over to his truck and drove down the sandy road leading to the Cabin in the woods. As he undressed to shower before going to bed, he reflected on all that had happened since morning. It wasn't a typical Thanksgiving Day in more ways than one. Nothing had been the same. Normally, his mother would've required everyone to go around the table telling at least one thing for which they were thankful. He supposed she was too upset over her stove not working to think about all the good things in her life.

He realized that he, too, had spent far too much time dwelling on the negative instead of the positive.

Not once had he stopped to be thankful. As the warm water sprayed over his body, he said, "Thank you, Lord for an indoor bathroom." He thought of the many nights he had to shower in the makeshift shower his father had put up outside, near the privy in the woods.

CHAPTER 26

Maddie and Tina were on their way from Troy to Kilby Prison in Montgomery, Alabama, when Maddie began to question whether this was such a good idea. For Tina to see her daddy in prison garb and hear the clanging of bars could be terrifying. Too late now. If she dared mention turning around, Tina would rightly feel she was breaking another promise. The child had had too many adults in her short lifetime making promises that weren't kept.

But what about Beau? Maddie began to worry. What if he refused to see her? After all, their last conversation was heated. She was furious with him for drinking and driving, which resulted in his wife's death. What really angered her was the fact that he wouldn't admit to what he had done. If only he'd shown remorse.

He told her to get on with her life and forget about him. He said he didn't plan to waste time worrying about what she thought, and as far as he was concerned she could forget she had a brother.

Her stomach ached as she replayed every hostile word spoken between them, shortly before he was put on a prison van and sent away. Angry, she responded it wouldn't be hard to do. But she didn't mean a word of it. There hadn't been a single day that she didn't think about him, yet the bitter last words were tattooed on her brain. But regardless of what happened between her and her brother, Tina deserved to see her daddy. Maddie hoped that even if Beau refused to see her, the guards would accompany Tina to see her daddy. No way would Beau refuse to see his little girl. He adored his little Tina Ballerina, as he called her.

They arrived at nine-thirty, and Maddie took time to explain to Tina what to expect.

"I understand, Aunt Tina. I heard some people say my daddy killed my Mommy, but it's not true. He loved her. He didn't do anything wrong."

Maddie pressed her lips together. "Sweetheart, he's not here because he didn't do anything wrong. But I'm sure he's very sorry for what happened to your Mommy, and he didn't mean for things to turn out this way."

"You think he killed her, too, don't you? But he didn't. I know he didn't. Maybe the car turned over on her. Or maybe she ate something that made her die. I don't know what happened, but my daddy would never hurt my mommy."

Maddie was told to have a seat, and the prisoner would be

brought in. She expected to have to talk with him with bars separating them, but to her surprise, they brought him into the room where they had seated her. A guard stood nearby.

Her throat tightened upon seeing him.

Tina squealed, "Daddy, daddy!" He turned to the guard. "Please? Can I pick up my child?"

The guard shook his head. "No contact."

Tina said, "That's okay, daddy. Aunt Maddie 'splained to me that we can't hug but that I can throw you a hug. Like this!" She wrapped her little arms around her body, then quickly propelled them forward toward her father. "Did you catch my hug?"

He laughed. "I sure did, my Tina Ballerina. Now, see if you can catch mine."

Maddie had sat quietly, and Beau had made no effort to recognize her presence. Her voice quivered. "You look good, Beau."

"I'm doing okay. Thanks for bringing Tina. I've missed her so much."

Tina said, "Daddy, how much longer before you can come and get me?"

He smiled. "If things go the way I'm hoping, sweetheart, it won't be nearly as long as I thought when they brought me here."

Maddie's forehead creased. "Are you serious?"

He nodded. "There's been a new wrinkle."

"What do you mean?"

"I can't tell you here, but hopefully, you'll hear about it soon."

Tina said, "Daddy, you didn't kill Mommy, did you?"

He shook his head. "No, baby. You know I would never do that."

"See, Aunt Maddie. I told you."

Beau frowned. "You told her I killed Trish?"

"No. She said she heard people accusing you, but she knew you had done nothing wrong. All I said was that you weren't in prison for not doing something wrong, but that you were very sorry and that you didn't mean for things to turn out this way."

"So, in other words, you told her I killed her mother."

"No, I didn't, Beau."

"But you believe it, don't you?"

Maddie glanced at Tina, who appeared to be taking in every word. "We don't need to have this conversation."

He nodded. "I agree." He said, "Tina Ballerina, can you still dance on your toes like a real ballerina?"

She giggled. "I can do it better now. She stood on her toes and pivoted. See?"

"Wow, you look like a real ballerina."

"Aunt Maddie bought me some real ballerina shoes. They have steel in the toes and they're pink. I wish I had brought them so you could see."

"Well, God willing, it won't be long before you can show them to me at home."

Tina was whirling around, when Maddie whispered, "It's wrong to get her hopes up, Beau."

166

"What's wrong with having hope, Maddie?"

"I don't want to see her let down."

"And you think I do?"

"What did you mean when you said there was a new wrinkle? New evidence?"

"What do you care? You're so sure I'm guilty, why does it matter to you?"

The guard announced visiting hours were over and Tina threw her daddy a big hug. "See you soon, Daddy."

He feigned a smile and returned her hug. "Yeah, baby. Real soon."

It was almost lunch time, and Maddie worried that Tina had her heart set on having turkey for Thanksgiving. She recalled seeing a Morrison's Restaurant near the mall and felt surely they'd have turkey with all the trimmings on the menu. But Maddie soon realized Tina was still giddy from visiting her dad and nothing could ruin her day. She ordered a fried chicken leg and a slice of blueberry pie with ice cream.

By the time they reached Troy, Tina Ballerina had fallen asleep in the car. Maddie picked her up, took her inside the apartment and laid her in the bed to finish her nap.

Exhausted, more from the emotional toll the trip had taken on her than the physical toll, her mind was scrambled. Was Beau lying to Tina when he said he didn't kill Trish? He had told Maddie the same thing just before being taken to prison, but the evidence was all there. There were only two of them in the car, the driver, and the passenger. He was the driver and Trish was the passenger. He survived. Trish died. Three witnesses on three separate vehicles testified to seeing him swerve all over the road, minutes before the fatal crash. The police officer wrote on the report that an open container of alcohol was found in the car. The report also said Beau was drunk and unable to walk a straight line.

Did he honestly believe he could change his story at this late date and fool anyone into believing him? *Oh, Beau. Why did you do it? What's gonna happen to Tina?*

Tina! Maddie's heart pounded. For months Maddie had assumed that she and Deuce would become foster parents. She knew Beau would never agree to adoption, but in ten years, when Beau was due to be released, Tina would be sixteen and capable of choosing where she wanted to live. But now that Maddie had broken up with Deuce in order to follow her dream, she realized that her dream didn't include taking on a dependent.

Maddie took out her movie projector and used the living room wall as a screen to watch a couple of women's college basketball games to help her memorize the plays. When the phone rang, she turned off the projector. Her pulse raced, when she realized it was Coach Weeks on the other end of the line.

The coach apologized to Maddie once again for missing the appointment and was confirming the interview for December 3rd. Maddie was confident that the job was in her pocket.

When Tina awoke, she wanted to play Old Maid, and after

that, she wanted Maddie to read her a story.

After talking with the Coach, Maddie was more eager than ever to review the ballgames, but Tina wasn't interested. She wanted to make cookies.

"Sweetheart, Aunt Maddie is tired, and I really need to watch some movies."

"Okay, will you make some popcorn, and we'll watch them together."

Maddie agreed, assuming Tina was tired and would go to sleep in her lap, since the games weren't likely to interest her more than a few minutes. After pouring the popcorn in a bowl, she turned on the projector and held out her arms for Tina to sit in her lap.

Tina shook her head and whimpered. "Not that movie. I want you to watch one with me on television."

Maddie turned on the TV and Tina seemed delighted that *I Love Lucy* was on. But in less than ten minutes, she was sound asleep on the sofa. Maddie picked her up and laid her in the bed. She dressed for bed and laid down beside her, too exhausted to do anything else. What had given her the idea that she could be content as a housewife and mother? Realizing how close she came to making a terrible mistake, caused her to break out in a cold sweat.

****

Tina woke Maddie up at six-fifteen Friday morning, crying.

Maddie rubbed her eyes and sat up in the bed. "What's wrong, sweetheart? Did you have a bad dream?"

She shook her head.

"Tell me why you're crying."

"I want my daddy."

Maddie sat on the side of the bed and held her in her arms. "I know you do. And Aunt Tina wishes he could be with you. But I'll take you back to see him again one day."

"When?"

"I can't say when, but I promise I will."

"I want to go home."

"To your house where you lived before the accident?"

"No. To where I live."

Maddie's brow lifted. "Oh! Okay. I'll take you back as soon as we can get dressed and eat breakfast. Is that what you want?"

She wiped her tears and nodded.

After Maddie walked her to the door of the Children's Home and left, guilt swept over her. How could she blame Tina for not wanting to stay another minute? Although she'd gone through the motions of catering to Tina's demands and had played cards, read stories, and even baked cookies with her, Maddie realized she'd gone through the motions, but her heart wasn't in it. Her mind had been preoccupied with her own wants and desires. She hadn't fooled Tina. No wonder the kid was ready to leave.

CHAPTER 27

Peggy had pulled some dumb stunts in her life, but trying to find out how Joel felt about her by insisting he date Darla was about the craziest idea she'd ever come up with. Her heart broke into a thousand pieces every time she saw them together.

Even if she hadn't been in love with Joel, to fix him up with Darla Grady would have been wrong in so many ways. They were nothing alike. Darla was a very independent woman. Not that being independent was a bad thing. It wasn't. There were times when Peggy wished to be more like her.

But Joel was old-school. He enjoyed opening doors for women, holding their umbrella for them, or letting them off in front of the door to keep them from having to walk across a gravel parking lot. He wanted to pay the bill at the restaurant and help his date with her coat. Perhaps Peggy knew him better than anyone, and she'd often been the recipient of his old-fashioned, gentlemanlike ways.

Darla, on the other hand took pride in what she described as "being on equal footing with a man." She bristled at the thought of being seen as the weaker sex. Peggy recalled hearing her snarky-sounding comment to the janitor, who made the mistake of holding a door for her. After such a sharp reprimand, Peggy had serious doubts that he'd ever want to do it again for any woman.

She groaned. If only she had dropped the idea after she first suggested to Joel that he date Darla. She was thrilled that he didn't appear interested. But she didn't drop it. Wanting to prove to herself that Darla's beauty hadn't turned his head, she brought it up again, hoping it would encourage him to compare the virtues of them both. Now, unfortunately, she realized that he *had,* and she was the one who came out on the short end, while Darla was out enjoying his company.

Darla began to show up at the office around closing time every afternoon. She had a habit of pulling up a chair next to Peggy's desk, for no other purpose than to brag about all the fun places Joel was taking her. It wasn't hard to tell that she was smitten.

She said, "Peggy, I can't thank you enough for getting us together. We're perfect for one another and I'm learning so much about him. I never dreamed he'd enjoy going to the Opera, but whenever I told him how much I wanted to see The Nutcracker in Birmingham, would you believe he found two tickets? He tries so hard to make me happy."

Peggy nodded. "That sounds like him."

"One of the things I love about him, is that I don't intimidate him, and that's a good thing. I suppose that's one reason I've never married. Most men I date, disappear after the first three months. They aren't confident enough in themselves and become intimidated by me. But not Joel. He allows me to be me. I let him know from our first date that I'm not some weak little female, needing a man, and I don't like to be treated as such. And you know what? He's good with that, but I'm sure I'm not telling you something you don't know, since you work closely with him."

Joel walked out, with his jacket slung over his shoulder. "I didn't hear you come in. Are you ready?"

"Yes, darling, and we need to hurry. I've made reservations for us at the Chinese Restaurant."

He groaned. "Chinese? Really?"

"Honey, I know you've made up your mind that you don't like Chinese food, but it's only because you haven't known what to order in the past. I'll order for you, and I know you'll enjoy whatever I choose for you. I plan to help you expand your palate preferences to include more than boring dishes like steak, roast beef, and pork chops."

Peggy turned to watch as Darla stepped in front of Joel to grab the door. Maybe she had him pegged all wrong. He didn't seem to mind at all, falling behind a strong woman who could open her own doors.

CHAPTER 28

It was December 3rd, the day of the long awaited interview. Maddie thought it would never come. She was up at four-thirty Friday morning. It had been an unusually warm November in Troy, but finally there was a chill in the air, with the weather man promising cold weather was on the way.

She was glad it would be cool enough for the orange sweater and corduroy skirt. She had tried on her skirt and sweater a dozen times in the past week and loved them more each time. They were perfect. Professional, but not so girly that it made her look as if she might throw like a girl. Dressed and ready to go, she paced the floor, waiting for time to pass. Stopping back by the full-length mirror, she decided to pull her hair up in a French twist. Perhaps it would look more professional.

How she missed having Josie for a roommate. Josie could always give her advice on what clothes to wear, or how to wear her hair and makeup. She rubbed the pink lipstick from her lips and picked up the tube of Tangerine Kiss. Blotting her lips on a tissue, she stared at her image in the mirror. She liked the Tangerine Kiss much better, since it matched her jersey top.

Finally, it was time to leave. A week ago, the weather was quite cold, but today she could get by without a jacket. Maybe she'd go by the University Bookstore after the interview and purchase an Auburn jacket.

On second thought, why buy one? She'd be given a special Coach jacket as soon as she got the job.

She arrived at the University twenty-five minutes early and waited in her car in front of the gym. She didn't want to be too early and appear over-anxious, but neither did she want to be late. At exactly five minutes 'til, she got out of the car and straightened her skirt. She knocked on the door, and Coach Weeks immediately invited her in.

She said, "And you are Maddie Anderson. I'm so glad to finally meet you. The entire coaching staff at Troy speaks very highly of you."

"Thank you. That's good to hear."

"I apologize again for being a no-show for our last appointment."

"I understand. That's quite alright."

"Good. Maddie, I want you to understand that I've agonized over the decision I've had to make. We narrowed the list of candidates down to two. It was between you and Rebekah

Rawlins."

Maddie smiled. "I'm flattered to be considered in the same category as Rebekah. She's very good."

"Yes, she is. That's why after several meetings this past week and much discussion we have decided to add her to our staff."

Maddie felt as if she couldn't breathe. "Does that mean—?"

Coach Weeks nodded. "I'm afraid so. I am truly sorry. We only came to a conclusion last night and I debated whether I should tell you on the phone or wait and tell you in person. It seemed unfair not to tell you face-to-face and to let you know that we will keep an eye on you. Coaches come and go. If and when we have another opening, if you are still interested in coming to the Plains, we'll keep your file handy." She stood. "Again, I'm very sorry. I hope you'll have a long and rewarding career, and I regret it won't be here."

Maddie felt as if she were in a daze as she walked back to her car. How could this have happened? She'd been so sure that the job was hers. It wasn't fair. She cried all the way back to Troy. *What now?*

She'd looked forward to the tournament coming up next week, but now after having her heart broken, it was hard to get excited over anything. She pulled off her new outfit. Little good it did. She could've worn a croaker sack and Coach Weeks wouldn't have noticed. Sure, Rebekah Rawlins had been coaching much longer than Maddie—and she was good—But she's no better than me. *They lost their last game, when it should've been a blowout. What was it that made Auburn choose her over me?*

After moping around all afternoon, Maddie popped some popcorn that evening and turned on the television to see a much-advertised made-for-television movie—A Charlie Brown Christmas. If anything could perk her up, that should do it. Knowing how much Deuce loved the Charlie Brown cartoons, she wondered if he'd be watching.

It was difficult keeping her mind on the movie, for wondering about Deuce. Did he miss her? Probably not, since he stayed so busy trying to do his work and the bookkeeper's also. She began to feel weepy, and it had nothing to do with getting the boot. There had been very little time lately to think about Deuce, but she suddenly felt extremely lonely.

After the big letdown, Maddie was convinced she'd never coach anywhere other than at a mediocre high school. Her high expectations had caused her to give up the best thing that had ever happened to her. Would living in Jinx Bay be so terrible, if she could be married to the love of her life?

She picked up the phone to call Deuce, but then placed her finger on the button to hang up, before she even finished dialing. Now was not the time to tell him. With the tournament coming up, she'd be terribly busy. No, she needed to wait until afterward, when she could drive down and talk to him in person. She'd let him know that she understood why he couldn't take off in April. As long as he could come home to her every night, she'd be content.

She'd send out resumes to neighboring schools. Surely, the fact that Auburn even considered her for a coaching position, would mean a lot on a resume. She'd apply at the Junior College. It wasn't so far that she couldn't make the drive every day.

CHAPTER 29

December 7th

Deuce had to drag himself to the town meeting, Tuesday night. Several times, he thought of making an announcement that he was resigning as City Council President. He had no business accepting it in the first place. But once he got there and sensed the excitement in the room, he didn't dare put a damper on their enthusiasm. Surely he could wait it out and resign after the first of the year.

The committees had all worked very hard, and everyone had been asked to bring a sample of what they'd be offering for sale. Lance had set up eight-foot tables all over the Conference room, and each table had an assortment of hand-made items. There were birdhouses, aprons, jewelry, paintings, fig preserves, hand-made tools, pottery, a colorful afghan and a platter of sliced Red Velvet Cake, which Granny said was a sample of the kind of bakery items available at their tent.

When Deuce asked for committee reports, Merle said she and her friends Betty and Lorene had ordered large rolls of beautiful Christmas paper and colorful ribbons. They planned to have a booth and would charge a nominal fee to gift wrap. "We'll wrap anything they choose to buy at the Festival, but they can also bring things they've purchased elsewhere, and we'll wrap it for them."

Marti reported that she and Candy were very pleased with the way the Christmas Pageant was shaping up. "The kids have all learned their parts, and we appreciate all the help the mothers have given us. The costumes look great, and the children couldn't be more excited."

Deuce said, "You ladies possibly have the most difficult job of all. I'm sure it hasn't been easy getting kids to settle down long enough to practice a play."

Candy said, "One might think so, but it hasn't been that way at all. They've been a real joy."

Marti cut her eyes at Deuce, then back to Marti. She said, "I'm so sorry to have to leave before we've been adjourned, but Deuce, Candy rode with me. Would you mind giving her a ride home after the meeting?"

Candy whispered, "What's wrong, Marti? Are you sick? Do you need me to go home with you?"

"No."

Deuce said, "I'm sorry you aren't feeling well. I'll be happy to take her home. It's on my way."

After everyone packed up their samples, Granny proudly announced she had no samples left to take home. Deuce was certain her heart would've been broken if there had been a tiny slice left.

Candy helped Deuce straighten the chairs after the room cleared out. She said, "I'm worried about Marti. Whatever she has, seems to have come on her quickly. I heard on the radio that there's a flu bug going around."

Deuce walked her to his truck, but had to put a clipboard, a jacket and two books in the back of the truck, in order for her to have a place to sit down. "Excuse the mess, but I'm not accustomed to having passengers." He opened the truck door and helped her as she stepped up on the running board. He said, "I would've cleaned it up if I had known I'd have the pleasure of escorting you home."

Her eyes twinkled when she smiled. "You're sweet, but it's fine. I appreciate the ride."

Her comment made him laugh. "Sweet? Is that what you called me?"

"You act as if I've insulted you. It was meant as a compliment."

"Well, I thank you ma'am. I'll take it as such, but I'm not sure anyone has ever used that term to describe me."

"Then they don't know you as well as I do."

"You think you know me, do you?"

"Absolutely."

"And what's your conclusion?"

"You remind me of a song."

"Oh yeah? And what song would that be?"

"The Great Pretender."

He laughed out loud, then belted out a few of the lyrics of a song sung by The Platters. "I seem to be . . . what I'm not, you see . . ."

Candy joined him. . . "You're wearing your heart like a crown."

Then he sang the next line: "I'm pretending that you're—." He stopped.

She said, "Did you forget the words? It's 'I'm pretending that you're still around'."

He turned to look at her. Their gaze locked. "I didn't forget."

Her nose crinkled. "What's wrong?"

"But you *are* still around. I've been too preoccupied with hurt pride to realize what was right in front of me."

Tears came in her eyes. "No, Deuce. I'm not her. I have a feeling you're missing your fiancé, but I'm no substitute."

He made no comment, which made Candy wonder if his silence indicated that he realized she was right. He pulled up and parked in front of #3 on Cannery Road. Then, eyeing the two cars and an ambulance parked in front of Mr. Lopez's cabin, he said, "Excuse me, Candy. I need to walk over and see what's going on."

"I'd like to go with you. Mr. Lopez is a sweet neighbor of

mine. I've been taking him a few meals and getting his mail for him. He hasn't been doing well lately. It looks like his friends may have called an ambulance to take him to the hospital."

"I didn't realize you two had met."

Just as they walked into the yard, two men came out holding a stretcher. A sheet was pulled over Mr. Lopez's face.

Deuce broke down and sobbed. Embarrassed, he, mumbled something to Candy, rushed over to his truck and hurriedly drove away.

Candy walked back to her own cottage, crawled into bed, pulled the covers over her head, and wept bitterly. "If only I could have a do-over, Lord. I'd do it all differently."

****

Deuce called his father as soon as he arrived back at the cabin in the woods and told him Mr. Lopez had died. Ronald said Mr. Lopez had been a very faithful employee for many years and he'd notify the funeral home to let them know he'd be responsible for burial expenses. He said, "Hold on. Your mother has something she needs to ask you."

Ramona got on the phone. "Deuce, I was standing nearby and heard you tell your father about poor Mr. Lopez. I know how much you loved him, but Ronald always goes by to see about him when he's in Jinx Bay, and he's told me that he's suffered a lot of pain in the past year. Now, he's free of pain and can join his wife and daughter."

"I know, Mom. You're right. I know he was ready to go."

"Well, that wasn't really what I wanted to talk to you about. I sent out invitations today for our annual Christmas Dinner, but if there's anyone you'd like to add to the list, I'll have room for two more people at the table if there's someone special you'd like to invite."

"Thanks, but I can't think of anyone, but if someone comes to mind, I'll give you a call."

"That's fine. We don't have to have every chair filled, but I'd hate to leave someone out that might not have a place to go."

"Hold on. I've just thought of someone. My new secretary is from Tampa, and she has indicated that she won't be going home before Christmas. You plan to have the dinner the weekend before. Right?"

"That's right. What's her name?"

"Candy. Candy McCoy. And she's become close friends with Marti Thompson, a schoolteacher. Maybe they could come together."

"Excellent. Give me their address and I'll mail them an invitation."

Deuce said, "Candy lives in Cottage #3 on Cannery Road. I don't have Marti's address. Just include her invitation in with Candy's."

When she hung up, Ronald said, "Did I understand you to say that Deuce has invited someone to the Christmas dinner?"

"Yes, his secretary and a friend of hers."

He looked surprised. "Betsy?"

"No. Apparently he has a new secretary. Her name is Candy."

He rubbed his chin. "Hmm . . . I don't know anyone in Jinx Bay by that name. She must be from out of town."

"I suppose."

"I heard you say there were two spots available."

"Not now. If his lady friends come, we'll have eight at the table. You, me, and Deuce make three, then there's Joel and Peggy, who make it five."

Ronald chuckled.

She said, "What's so funny?"

"The way you linked Joel and Peggy's name together. Honey, will you ever give up? They are coworkers, not lovers."

"I know that. You asked how many have been invited, and I was simply giving you a count."

"Okay, I'm sorry. So, that's five, and Deuce's two friends make seven. But you said eight."

"That's right. I sent Maddie an invitation."

"Oh. I didn't realize Deuce had asked you to invite her."

"He didn't have to."

Ronald's forehead creased into a frown. "Are they still together? I haven't heard him say."

"Have you heard him say that they aren't together?"

He lifted a shoulder in a shrug. "Now that you mention it, I don't suppose I have. I just had the idea that they had broken up. But I'm glad to know I was wrong. I like Maddie."

CHAPTER 30

December 13, 1965
Eufaula, Alabama

Monday morning Peggy was dressing for work and thought it strange that Joey was still asleep, but it gave her extra time to change clothes three times. Why should she bother? It wasn't as if she were trying to impress anyone. Finally, deciding on a white sweater and cardigan with her red skirt, she finished primping, then went in to wake the baby.

When she picked him up, he wasn't his usual happy self. In fact, he almost appeared lethargic. She tried to dismiss it as lack of sleep, since he often would wake up and play in his bed instead of falling back to sleep. But when he wouldn't take his bottle, she became worried. She carried him back to the nursery, dressed him, then picked up the phone and called Joel to tell him she planned to take Joey to see the pediatrician.

He said, "Maybe he's teething and doesn't feel like sucking on his bottle. Does he have a temperature?"

"I don't think so. And maybe you're right. He has been trying to cut a tooth. I'm sure that's it. I hate to carry him in a waiting room full of sick kids. If he's not sick now, he will be for sure if he's exposed to every virus going around."

"Don't worry about coming in. I understand what you're saying about the exposure, but I really think you should take him to see the doctor. It won't hurt to have him checked out to relieve your mind."

"Thanks. I suppose you're right. I will."

"Give me a call and let me know after you find out something."

Peggy was surprised at how quickly she got in to see the pediatrician. In less than thirty minutes, she was called to the back. She began by making an apology for taking up his time, since she was sure there was nothing seriously wrong but—

He said, "Slow down. You did the right thing by bringing him here."

When she started to question whether he had a valid reason for making such a statement, he held up his palm, as to say, "no questions."

She watched Joey's reaction as the doctor talked to him and let him play with the stethoscope. He looked normal, yet she had an unexplainable feeling that the doctor was seeing something that troubled him. Was it her imagination?

He said, "He's very thin."

"He's getting taller. I think it makes him look skinny."

"I'd like to run a few tests on Joey."

"What kind of tests? Why? What are you looking for?"

"Don't panic. It's all exploratory to make sure we haven't missed something. While we have him in here, it's a good time to have it done."

She breathed a little easier, hearing his explanation.

The nurse came in, picked Joey up and the doctor told Peggy it wouldn't take long. She was always amazed that Joey never met a stranger, and she was especially glad at times like these whenever she couldn't go with him. It had made it much easier for her to go to work, since she couldn't have stood it if he cried whenever she had to leave him.

When the nurse brought him back, she told Peggy the doctor would send her the results of the tests within a few days, but that she shouldn't worry. He gave her something to rub on Joey's gums.

"Is that all he said?"

"Yes ma'am. I wouldn't worry. Teething can cause a baby to be irritable and have stomach problems."

Peggy walked out. He was neither irritable, nor did he have stomach problems. True, he was teething, but the doctor didn't have to run tests to discover that fact. What was he looking for?

She took the remainder of the day off, as Joel had suggested.

She watched little Joey all afternoon, searching for signs of something that could've given the doctor a reason for wanting to run the tests. She wished now that she had asked more questions.

Four days passed and Peggy still hadn't heard from the doctor. She convinced herself that it was a good sign—that there was nothing to tell. But that afternoon, she received a call from the receptionist saying that Dr. Strickland wanted her to come in for a consultation at four-thirty.

"But I don't know a Dr. Strickland. That isn't my doctor."

"He's a pediatric cardiologist."

"Did you say a cardiologist?" When Peggy pressed her for a reason for the appointment, she hedged, saying she wasn't privy to the information. She said any questions that Peggy had could be addressed by Joey's pediatrician. Yet, when she asked to speak to him, she was told he was unavailable.

It was a long day, as Peggy's thoughts carried her down countless frightening scenarios. At four o'clock she walked into Joel's office. "I'm leaving now, for the consultation."

"Would you like for me to pick up Joey for you at the sitter's?"

"No, thank you. I called and she said it would be fine to leave him until I get back from the doctor's office. I'm worried, Joel. I don't know the doctor who has set up the appointment. I'm told that he's a cardiologist. That means they think there's something wrong with my baby's heart, doesn't it?" Tears welled in her eyes.

"Peggy, I suspect they may have found some type of an abnormality, but even if they have, it doesn't mean a death sentence. I had heart surgery when I was sixteen months old and I'm healthy as a horse." He winked. "Well, maybe a geriatric horse."

"You aren't serious."

"I am. I had something called Atria Ventricular Canal Defect." He smiled. "Now, look at me. The only problem I have is trying to make my secretary smile."

"Thank you. You're doing great, but I'm too nervous to smile."

He stood, picked up his coat from the back of his chair, and said, "Wait. I want to go with you."

"That's not necessary."

"I know. But I want to be there for Frank."

"For Frank?"

"Yes. We had our differences at times, but it was only whenever I began to act so irresponsible and do things to hurt people. I don't blame him for wanting to bash my head in. He should have. But he was my friend, even when we stopped seeing eye-to-eye. He can't be here for you today, but I know he'd want someone to be with you, even if it's me."

"You knew him well. Thank you, Joel. I'll meet you at the hospital."

"Better still, you come ride with me. After the office visit, I'll bring you back here to pick up your car."

Joel escorted Peggy into the hospital and was sent upstairs to the cardiologists office. As soon as Peggy registered, she and Joel were ushered into a plush office. They were told Dr. Strickland would be in shortly.

Peggy looked around at the various diplomas and awards lining the walls.

Hearing her teeth chatter, Joel took her hand and whispered, "You're nervous. I understand. I'm sorry you're having to wait."

"I am nervous, but my teeth are chattering because it's freezing in here."

He pulled off his sport coat and hung it around her shoulders. Then, the door opened, and a tall, slender man walked in, extended his hand, and introduced himself as Dr. Maloy.

This time, Peggy decided the chattering of teeth wasn't from the temperature. From the look on the doctor's face, he had not come into the room bearing good news. Joel reached over and squeezed her hand. She could tell he was nervous also.

Strange how Joel could've become so attached to Joey. Perhaps he'd always had a special place for children in his heart. She'd never had the opportunity to observe him around any other kids.

From the doctor's strange demeanor, Peggy got the idea he was angry. But why? Hadn't she done everything exactly the way Joey's pediatrician had suggested?

CHAPTER 31

The doctor wasted no time before getting down to the facts. He said, "This child should've been evaluated at birth and scheduled for heart surgery before leaving the hospital when he was born. It should be normal procedure in Down Syndrome cases, since half the children with Down Syndrome are born with Atria Ventricular Canal defect. Surgery is successful in the majority of cases, when detected early. Surely, you were told this. What possessed you to wait until now?"

Peggy's lip quivered. She was right. He was angry. Her voice quaked. "Early? How early?"

"Typically, we like to do the surgery within the first four to six months of life. I don't understand why this child wasn't brought in earlier."

Peggy decided now was not the time to explain that Joey was in an institution at that stage in his life. What good would it do?

The doctor ranted. "He has all the symptoms. Didn't you question why his nails have a bluish tint? Surely, you didn't think it was normal."

Peggy broke down in sobs.

Joel said, "Doc, I believe you're coming down hard on the wrong person. This is her first baby, and the fact that Joey has Down Syndrome makes it difficult to know what's normal for a Down Syndrome child, when compared to a normal child. I saw the tint in his nails, too, but assumed it was a symptom associated with his condition."

Peggy said, "It's too late to change the past. What are his chances now? Will he—? Is he gonna—?" Her voice broke.

The doctor said, "I understand your frustration. And if you're trying to ask if his condition is fatal, I wouldn't be able to answer that question." He reached over and laid his hand on her arm. "Ma'am, all my patients are going to die."

Her eyes widened. "What? Then what are we doing here?"

Joel said, "Pardon me doc, but this mama is not in the mood for jokes. She's scared to death, and rightfully so."

"You're right. I apologize. I came in here frustrated that this child is eighteen-months-old, with Down's Syndrome and yet he's never even been evaluated for a hole in his heart. I realize that I was passing my frustrations on to you all, and attempted to lighten things up a bit, but it backfired. The truth is, I can give you hope, but I can't give you guarantees."

Joel said, "I was born with AV Canal defect, and had surgery

194

at sixteen months. I was told not to participate in rough sports, but I played basketball, and the coach would take me out when he saw I was getting winded. I've never had a problem."

The doctor raised a brow. "That's very interesting. But I don't understand why you withheld that information."

"Withheld? I wasn't withholding anything. No one asked. Why does it matter?"

"That's more reason than ever why Joey should've been diagnosed before now."

"What do you mean?"

"It's not always, but AVCD can be genetic. Since he's Down Syndrome and his father was born with the same defect, he was bound to have it."

Joel shook his head. "But I'm—" He turned and glared at Peggy. When she lowered her head, he knew. But why was he just now finding out? Why had she lied to him?

The doctor waited. "You were saying?"

"I think I just lost my train of thought."

"Very well. I'd like to have Joey here Thursday morning at six o'clock. Surgery will be scheduled at seven. The nurse will be in shortly with a list of do's and don'ts. If you have questions in the meantime, don't hesitate to call my office."

Joel and Peggy walked out, got on the elevator, lumbered down a long hall, went out the door, got into the car, and drove away without a single word between them.

He drove her back to the office to where her car was located. "Before you get out, isn't there something you failed to tell me?"

"No."

"Don't lie to me, Peggy. He's mine, isn't he?"

Her chin trembled.

He threw his head back with his eyes closed. "I had no idea. Why? Why didn't you tell me?"

"You want to know why? Really? I'll tell you why, Joel. You knew I was pregnant when you decided to divorce me. Remember what you told me? In case you don't, let me refresh your memory. You said, 'Since we are dissolving the marriage, you need to dissolve that thing inside you.' *That thing*. That's exactly what you called my baby. *My* baby, Joel. *My* baby. You gave up all rights to him the minute you instructed me to do away with him."

"Oh, Peggy, Peggy, Peggy. I was so messed up at that time of my life. You know I didn't know what I was saying. I beg of you. Please don't shut me out of my son's life."

"Begging doesn't become you, Joel. So, don't. I'll admit you aren't the same man you were then, but Frank married me, knowing I was carrying your child. As far as I'm concerned, Joey is a Jinright. Frank was thrilled to have him carry his name."

"Peggy, you're denying me my child out of spite. I did you wrong in the past. I admit it. I've begged you to forgive me, and I truly thought you had. I know now, it wasn't real. You still hate me. But please, I beg you, do anything to me you want, but please, please don't deny me my own flesh and blood."

"Goodbye, Joel."

"Goodbye? Are you saying you won't be working for me anymore?"

Her eyes squinted into tiny slits as if she were mulling over the question. "No. I need the job. I'll continue to work at Garrison & Gunter, but our relationship will strictly be on a professional level."

CHAPTER 32

Maddie had moped around for days, but after receiving an invitation from Deuce's mother to the family Christmas Dinner, all her fears were dispelled. She wanted to call Deuce, but after calling Josie and telling her all about her big disappointment, she said, "Josie, to be honest, I think I got carried away with the idea that I could be somebody special."

Josie said, "But you are somebody, Maddie. Don't sell yourself short just because you got turned down on a single interview."

"You know what I mean. But I've come back down to earth, and I know what I really want, now, and it's Deuce."

"Are you sure you aren't settling?"

"What do you mean?"

"Since you didn't get what you want, you're now willing to settle on the second best thing? That's so wrong, Maddie. It's wrong to do Deuce that way, but it's wrong for you, too."

Maddie had always respected Josie's counsel, but this time it rubbed against the grain. "You're wrong, Josie. I wasn't thinking straight. I've loved Deuce from the first night we met, and that's the truth. Even before I agreed to go on the interview, I told you that I loved him. Surely, you remember me saying that."

"I remember. But when it came down to making a choice between the two, I know which one you chose. It's wrong, Maddie, to expect him to be forgiving. But what if he did forgive you and you go back to him and afterward another outstanding offer comes along? What will you do then?"

"I'll still choose Deuce. I didn't just call to tell you about losing the job offer. That was the bad news. The good news is that I've been invited to have Christmas Dinner with Deuce and his family and a few of their close friends. We'll have a chance to clear the air."

"Well, that changes things."

"What do you mean?"

"I figured after you wrote Deuce that 'Dear John Letter,' you felt as if you had him on a string, and since the job didn't pan out, you felt you could pull him back into your boat at will. I was afraid you were wrong, and that he'd not be so willing to forgive you for dumping him. I wanted to save you the humiliation.

But the fact that he's invited you to the Christmas Dinner

means he must love you very much and has forgiven you."

"I have no doubts. He's so sweet, Josie. I can't even fathom how I could've ever thought coaching would make me happier than spending my life with Deuce."

Wednesday afternoon was the first night of the women's basketball tournament in the gym. They had to be finished and out by six-fifteen for the men's team to practice. Maddie no longer fretted over the inequality that existed when it came to the public holding the men's team with such high esteem while pooh-poohing at women who enjoyed the same sport.

One day, things would be different, and in the meantime, she'd continue to enjoy coaching and choose to be grateful that it didn't consume her life. She loved the sport, but it wasn't her only love. If she wound up having to coach young girls in her backyard at Jinx Bay, so be it. But wherever she was planted, she would never stop promoting the idea of women's sports filling gyms and stadiums with thousands of eager fans, cheering for their favorite team.

CHAPTER 33

Candy McCoy called her friend Marti and asked if she minded giving her a ride to the Christmas Festival Planning Meeting.

"I'll be happy to. I'll be there in ten minutes."

When she drove up in front of Cabin #3, the first thing she noticed was Candy's car was missing. She didn't think much of it, since she presumed such a fine car deserved to be serviced regularly and was probably in the shop. But when Candy came walking out, Marti sensed there was something wrong. But when Candy didn't mention anything, Marti decided if Candy wanted her to know, she'd tell her. They talked about the play, and what all had been accomplished in such a short length of time. Just before reaching the church, Candy said, "Thank you, Marti."

"For what?"

"For being such a good friend."

"I think it's the other way around. I need to thank you. I'll hate for these practices to end. I've enjoyed working together."

"Me too. But remember what you said about believing God put us together . . . or something to that affect. How did you state it?"

"I said I believe God has put you in my life for a reason. I still do. Now, whether we've achieved that goal or whether it's yet to be played out, I can't say. But I'm still convinced that God had a purpose for getting us together. Maybe it's for your sake, maybe for mine. Or how nice it would be if it's to draw us both closer to the Lord."

Candy's eyes brightened. "I think I know what it's all about."

"That's great. Do you feel at liberty to share it with me, or is it too personal?"

Candy sat chewing on her bottom lip, as if contemplating an answer to a difficult question.

She nodded her head, "Yes." Then quickly she changed it to 'no.' "I mean yes it *is* personal, but no it isn't too personal to tell you. I want you to know. I've kept so many secrets for the past two years, and I've been afraid to share what's been going on in my life, for fear of the consequences. I suppose we should go in and get started. If you have time to go in the cottage with me after you take me home, I have a lot to unload on you."

The practice went great. Candy was so proud of the children and how hard they worked. It was fun helping design and sew the costumes. She was no seamstress, but she could sew two pieces of material together, and although it might not hold up for countless washings, it would do fine for three nights.

After rehearsal, Candy and Marti waited under the shelter for the parents to pick up the children. After the last one was picked up, they turned off the lights, locked the church doors and headed toward Cannery Road. Marti made a pot of coffee, then giggled.

Marti said, "You have a sneaky look on your face, like you have something up your sleeve."

She reached in the cabinet and pulled out a yellow Moon pie, which made Marti laugh.

"Not you, too!"

"I hadn't had a Moon Pie since I was a child until I went to your house the other night. It was so good, I went the day after and bought two boxes." She poured two cups of coffee and sat down at the kitchen table with Marti. Sucking in a deep breath, she said, "I suppose you noticed my T-Bird is gone."

"Gone? I saw it wasn't in your yard, but I assume it's at a dealership?"

Candy shook her head. "Nope. I went to Montgomery Thanksgiving, to see Jack."

Marti winced. "I see."

"No. You don't see but when I explain, I hope you'll understand why I did what I did. After you and I talked the other night, I went home, and I prayed and asked God to forgive me for the lies I told and the ones I lived out. I can't explain what happened or why I felt so strongly that I should give Jack back everything that I had taken from him. That included an emerald ring, a gold bracelet, and a red T-Bird. Those things were tangible. There was much more that I took from him that I had no way of giving back, but I had a peace about it."

"I suppose he was surprised."

"Probably not as surprised as I was. It's hard to explain, and I'm sure it's even harder for you to understand. But it was as if I were being maneuvered by a giant magnet held over my head, drawing me toward Montgomery. I almost felt it was out of my control. Yet, as much as I loved that car, it was easy handing over the keys, and I've had no regrets. Isn't that peculiar?"

"Not when it's being led by the Holy Spirit."

"Do you really think I was? Being led, I mean?"

"I can't say, Candy. Only God can reveal that answer to you, but I will say it does sound like a divine experience to me."

Her eyes popped wide open. "Yes, that's what it felt like. A divine experience. And you know what else happened that was strange? I picked up a Bible that someone named Gideon had left in the hotel, and I didn't know where to start reading. But I opened it, and began to read, and it was a story about a woman at the well. She sounded a lot like me. I loved the ending, when Jesus said, 'Go and sin no more.'"

"It's a beautiful story, for sure. I'm eager to know what Jack said about the change in you. I know he must've been shocked."

"He was. He didn't want to take the car or the jewelry. But we had a long talk, and I explained to him that I was wrong to do the things I did. I used him."

"I suppose. But think how he used you, Candy. He took advantage of you."

"He didn't do anything I didn't allow. I told him about meeting you, and how happy you seemed. I thought it was because you probably had everything you wanted. Then I came over and saw where you lived, and I told him about the old car you drive—"

Candy suddenly stopped and popped her hand over her lips. "Oh, Marti. I'm so sorry. I got so involved in explaining what happened between Jack and me, that I didn't realize how it must sound to you. I wasn't saying it to put you down. I was making a point that it wasn't material possessions that brought you joy."

"I'm not offended, Candy. I'm loving every minute of this conversation. Please don't stop."

"Good. Anyway, I guess I was on a roll. I told him about me telling you that I was bad because of the bad things I had done, and I told him what you said when I made the statement that you are good. Do you remember?"

She smiled. "Maybe not exactly, but I can imagine what I must've said."

"I know exactly. You said, 'I'm not good. But I'm Redeemed. It's Christ in me that's good.' Something happened to me at that moment. I wanted what you had. I wanted Christ to dwell in me."

"Do you think Jack understood what you were saying?"

"I know he did, because he sat quietly the whole time I was talking. Then when I finished, he said, 'Candy, it's I who owe you an apology. What you took from me was nothing compared to what I took from you.' His statement didn't make sense, because he was the one giving and I was the one taking. Then he said, 'What you took from me were things that could be replaced. I can buy another car, another ring, another bracelet. But it was cruel what I took from you.' I didn't understand, since I had nothing to give."

"Did he explain why he said it?"

"He did. He said, 'Candy, when you said you told your friend Marti you were 'bad, your words pierced my heart like a sharp knife. I realized you didn't have those thoughts when you began working for me. It wasn't until I stole your self-respect that you regarded yourself as worthless. I did that to you, and I am so sorry."

"It's okay Jack. I've been forgiven, and I forgive you."

"What did he say to that?"

Candy's voice quivered. "He said, 'I've felt for a long time that God was trying to get my attention, but I couldn't turn loose of the bitterness I harbored toward my ex-wife. I thought we had a good marriage—not great, but good.' Then, he said he discovered he was only fooling himself. His wife was sneaking around with his best friend.

Jack said he was terribly hurt, but he was also angry. Angrier than he'd ever been in his life. He said he wanted to get back at her and he thought the way to do it was to find someone younger and prettier to prove to her that she was replaceable. He said he took me to all the places he felt that either she or her friends would see us."

"Marti, you never asked why I left a good job to come here."

"I assumed it was because you realized what you were doing was wrong."

Candy shook her head. "I wish that had been the case. It wasn't. Jack sent me away. But I was okay with that, because he gave me $500, a T-Bird and expensive jewelry. He said he and his wife were getting back together.

But when we talked over Thanksgiving, he said the real reason he wanted me out of town and out of his life was because he was afraid God would strike him dead if he continued to see me. And he was afraid he wouldn't be able to stay away."

Marti said, "Do you think he was serious?"

Candy nodded. "I do. He said strange, unexplainable things had been happening in his life. I told him I understood. I've been praying for him. I thought he would laugh. Me? Praying? But he didn't. It was then that he told me about a recurring dream he had, where there were two forces fighting for his will."

"His will to do what?"

"To choose which side he was on. He said he'd always thought that he was too smart to be taken in by religion and felt ignorant people used God as a crutch. But then the dreams started. He described giant arms on two sides of him, pulling him in opposite directions. The dreams taunted him. He said he woke up in a sweat, night after night. Then, he said, 'I'm not afraid anymore, Candy. I know if you could come here on your own and hand me the keys to your car and tell me it's because of what God is doing in your life, then there's no denying it. It's real."

Marti said, "That's wonderful."

"But that's not all. Jack said, 'Candy, you're the real thing. Would you mind praying that God will do for me what he's done for you?'"

Marti began to cry. "So, what did you do?"

Candy lowered her head. "What do you think? I prayed, Marti. It's the first time I'd ever prayed out loud and at first I was self-conscious because when I prayed for myself there was no one listening but God. It was different, knowing Jack was hanging on to every word coming out of my mouth. I was intimidated, but it didn't last long. It was as if the Lord grabbed hold of my tongue and put the words in my mouth. When I finished praying, Jack hugged me. Not the way he once did. It was sweet. He thanked me for praying. Now, I can't say for a fact that God moved in his heart the way he's moved in mine, but I really do believe a change took place in his life."

"That's a wonderful testimony, Candy. I'm sorry you had to give up your car."

"I'm not. I wanted to get rid of everything that reminded me of my former lifestyle. I have, and now I can sing that little song you taught the children, 'I've got the joy, joy, joy, joy down in my heart . . . down in my heart to stay.'"

CHAPTER 34

The Jinx Bay City Council Conference Room was packed and unlike the first meeting, there was no squabbling. Everyone was excited and wanting to tell all the wonderful things they had experienced, working together. Neighbors who hadn't spoken in weeks, were now having their morning coffee together.

Deuce couldn't help thinking how close he came to throwing in the towel and saying he was too busy to spend time trying to play referee to a bunch of grumpy folks. Now, it was hard to imagine anyone in the room as being grumpy. Even Granny Noles had become lovable. He smiled. Perhaps she was lovable before, but the bitterness in his own heart kept him from seeing the good in people. He recalled cringing whenever she stood to speak—even trying to cut her off before she had her say. What a blessing the group had been.

He tapped his gavel on the podium. "I have something I'd like to say." He thanked them all for their hard work. "Tomorrow night all your efforts will pay off. Have your booths set up by three o'clock, and we'll open the festival to the public beginning at four. The fellows have done a great job of turning the Gazebo into a stable, and the Children's Live Nativity Pageant will do four continuous runs, to give everyone an opportunity to go by and enjoy their efforts."

Mildred raised her hand. "Don't you think four times is too much to expect of those kids? They're gonna get awfully tired, repeating their lines that many times. I think we should set a certain time for a single performance."

Candy stood. "I understand your concerns Mildred. I might've thought the same thing if I hadn't been working with the kids for weeks. Trust me, they are so excited and as some of you can attest, the word 'tired' isn't in their vocabulary. They love acting out the Christmas Story and would be thrilled to repeat it as long as anyone would stand and watch. They're the sweetest children and Marti has done such a great job with them."

Barbara Adams raised her hand. "I thank you both for all you've done. My Bradley is a handful. How you ever managed to get him interested is beyond me. He has an attention deficit disorder and can blank out everything going on around him. His grandfather taught him how to make paper airplanes, and it has become an obsession. I literally have to hide my books, because he tears out the pages and makes airplanes. I find them all over the house." She paused. Her face turned red. "I'm sorry, I didn't mean to go on and on."

Lance said, "You're doing great Barbara. We all love Bradley and are interested in hearing about him."

"Thank you. I just wanted to say that Bradley will be the one back of the curtain, holding the star. It's all he talks about now. He says, 'I'm the star that tells the shepherds where to find Jesus. Except for baby Jesus, I'm the most important one.'

Now maybe I should correct him and talk about being prideful, but to tell the truth, I think he's right. Participating in the pageant comes easy for some of these kids, but for my Bradley, it's a big deal. So, tomorrow night y'all might see the star bouncing up and down or swaying a bit, but I don't think it will ever be very far away from the baby Jesus. Bradley takes his part seriously. After all, he's the most important one, you know." She chuckled with tears muddling in her eyes.

The entire room rose to their feet and clapped.

Deuce concluded the meeting. Marti said, "Would you mind taking Candy home?"

"I'll be happy to. Is something wrong with her car?"

"I'll let her be the one to tell you. She rode here with me, but I want to run by the grocery store, and I thought you might be going her way."

"Sure. Where did she go?"

"I think Bradley's mother wanted to talk to her. She's the one who was responsible for getting through to Bradley about the importance of being the star. It seems there was a wall separating him from the other kids, and I don't know how Candy did it, but she tore down that wall."

He turned out the lights, locked the door and went outside, to find that no one had left, but were all gathered together, laughing, and sharing funny stories about their experiences. He walked up to Barbara, Bradley, and Candy. Bradley said, "Hey, Mr. Deuce. Did you know I'm gonna be the star that shines on Jesus?"

Deuce ran his fingers through the little snaggle-tooth child's hair. "I did know that buddy. You're gonna do great."

"It's easy. I just hold the stick that has a star on the end, and I make sure it's over the baby's head. My Grandpa's coming to watch me."

Barbara grinned. "He's right. And knowing my dad, the star is the only thing Bradley's grandpa will see. I can't tell you how much this means to our family."

When Barbara and Bradley walked away, Candy said, "I need to find Marti."

"Marti left ten minutes ago."

"I'm sure you're wrong. I came here with her. She wouldn't have left me."

"No, she didn't. She had an errand to run. I said I'd be happy to take you home."

She pursed her lips. "Are you sure that's how that conversation went?"

"Of course, I'm sure." He smiled. "Are you afraid of my driving?"

"No, but I hope I'm not putting you out."

"Keep up that kind of foolish talk, and I may be the one putting you out. Come on. I'm thinking a hot cup of cocoa would taste really good about now, and I'm not called the Cocoa King for nothing. Could I persuade you in letting me take you to my little corner of the world and proving to you that you've never had a cup of hot cocoa until you've tasted mine?"

"And where is your little corner of the world?"

His smile faded. "I was talking about my cabin, but if that makes you uncomfortable—"

She giggled. "I trust you, Deuce."

"Good."

Candy sipped on a cup of cocoa, and Deuce laughed when the marshmallow got on the tip of her nose. She affirmed it was the best she'd ever drank and that he indeed deserved the title of Cocoa King. They discussed everything that took place at the meeting. Then Deuce asked the question that had been on both their minds.

He said, "What's going on, Candy?"

"What did Marti tell you?"

"Absolutely nothing. But when I asked about your car, I got the distinct feeling there was something she knew that I didn't, but I also had the feeling that for some reason she thought I should." He shrugged. "I know that didn't make sense, but I'm having trouble trying to make sense of a lot of things."

"It makes perfect sense. I didn't know Marti planned to leave me so that you'd take me home, but I know why she did. Deuce, you think you know me, but you don't."

"I know enough about you to know that I think you're one of the sweetest girls I've ever known. I only wish I had met you a couple of years ago."

She rolled her eyes. "Me too. You don't know how much I wish that. But you go first. Why would two years have made a difference?"

"It would be before I met Maddie."

"Your fiancé?"

"She's no longer my fiancé."

"I'm sorry. When did this happen?"

He briefly shared with her about the letter, and Maddie choosing a career over marrying and moving to Jinx Bay. "But don't feel sorry for me. I'm glad it happened. It's better to find out now than for her to discover after the wedding that she wasn't cut out to live in a little fishing village, and this is my life. I'd never be happy working in an office in a city."

"I understand."

"Do you, really?"

"I do."

"Now, it's your turn. Why did you agree that it would've been better if we'd met a couple of years ago."

She stared into space. "Tighten your belt. This is gonna be a bumpy ride."

Deuce took a sip of cocoa. "I'm ready."

She found it difficult to look at him as she went through her whole life's history, from her childhood with a mother who was an addict, to the day she went to work for Jack. She'd glance up momentarily from time to time, trying to read his thoughts. Was he thoroughly disgusted with her for allowing Jack to use her in such a degrading way? Would he want to announce to the Christmas Committee that he made a terrible mistake by allowing her to work with kids? As the horrifying scenarios flashed through her mind, she lost her train of thought and burst into tears.

Deuce pushed back from the table and stood. "Get up."

She stood and headed toward the door. "I'm sorry, Deuce. I didn't set out to deceive you. Things got out of control, and it was being around Marti that made me see that I wasn't like her. I wondered why I was never happy, regardless of all the fine things Jack showered me with, yet Marti had so little in material goods, yet she was filled with such joy. I wanted what she had. I didn't care about cars or jewels or big bank accounts. I wanted peace."

He said, "I wish you could've come to me and told me what you're telling me now."

"I wanted to. Honest, I did. But by the time I admitted to myself what a shameful person I was, I had already fallen in love with you and couldn't bring—" Her throat tightened, and she closed her eyes tightly. "Oh, no. I can't believe I said that. I didn't mean it. I didn't, Deuce. I'm nervous and I don't know what I'm saying. Please take me home and I promise I'll take a bus out of town in the morning. You'll never have to see me again."

His chin quivered. "You did mean it. You love me, Candy."

"No. It came out wrong."

He stretched out his arms and gently wrapped them around her body. "Okay. You don't have to love me if you don't want to. But would you mind terribly if I told you I know for a certainty that I've fallen head over heels in love with you?"

She lifted her head. Their gaze locked. "You are? In love with me?"

"More than I ever thought possible."

She pushed away. "No. That's wrong, Deuce. You aren't really in love with me. You've been hurt by your fiancé, and you want to get back at her."

"That's not true. Maddie helped me to stop mourning over losing my teenage girlfriend. I began to laugh again, and it felt good. She's a sweet girl, and we had fun together, but I began to see weeks ago that we wanted different things in life. Doesn't mean she's wrong to want what she wants, or that I'm wrong for wanting what I want. But a marriage between us would've been a grave mistake. I'll admit, my pride was crushed when she sent me a Dear John letter." He chuckled. "To be truthful, I think I was irritated that I hadn't had the courage to end it and waited until she did."

"So, you really mean it? You love me? Even after all I've told you about myself?"

"Candy, I loved you before you came here tonight, but I was

in denial. I didn't think I was ready for love. I've been fooled before. I once convinced myself I was in love with Maddie, but the closer it came to April, the more I began to sweat. Don't get me wrong—I love Maddie—I'm just not IN love with Maddie.

I'm so glad you told me all about you and Jack. I know it wasn't easy, but if anything, it strengthened the love I feel for you. It's humbling to hear what God has been doing in and through you since you first arrived in Jinx Bay. You aren't just beautiful on the inside. You're beautiful all the way through. And I agree with your friend, Jack. Candy McCoy, you *are* the real thing."

CHAPTER 35

December 16th

Thursday morning Peggy Jinright arrived at the hospital with Joey at six o'clock and was ushered into a room. The nurse said they'd come for Joey shortly. Five minutes past six, Joel Gunter walked in. Peggy was sitting in a chair, holding a very sleepy little boy. She looked up. "What are you doing here?"

"I don't think you have to ask that question. You know why I'm here."

Joey had his head on his mommy's shoulder. Hearing Joel's voice, he raised his head, then smiling he turned and held out his arms.

Joel's gaze met Peggy's. "May I?"

She nodded slightly and he reached down and picked up Joey.

He asked, "Do you know anything, yet?"

"Only that they said he'll be taken back in a few minutes."

A doctor walked in with a nurse. The nurse took Joey from Joel and left the room. The doctor explained the surgery would take five or six hours, and that they'd use patches to repair the hole in his heart. But there was nothing new in what he said, since it was all explained in the eight pages of information they received on their last visit.

After he left, Joel said, "Why don't we go down to the cafeteria and eat breakfast."

Peggy's teeth ground together. Her arms were crossed over her chest. "I'm fine."

"Peggy, you can be angry at me for finding out that Joey is my son, and I can be angry at you for not telling me. But in a few minutes, our little boy will have his heart cut open and if all goes well, he'll come out alive. If something should go wrong, we won't have any reason to be angry any longer. So, why don't we reverse that situation? Let's form a bond while there's still hope for him. Let's lean on one another. Then if we should lose him, it won't matter to me if you're angry. You can hate me if you choose. Just stand with me for five or six hours. That's all I ask. Please?"

She stood and picked up her purse. "I am a bit hungry, but I really want a cup of hot coffee."

They went through the line at the cafeteria, and both ordered a hearty breakfast. When they sat down, Joel asked if she'd mind if he prayed.

At first, she suspected he was doing it to impress her. But hearing his heartfelt cry, she discerned that he'd been doing quite a bit of praying lately.

The wait was dreadfully long, but Peggy couldn't deny that it would've been much longer, had Joel not been there to help comfort her. After five hours, they received a call informing them that the surgery was going well, and that it should be finished in a couple of hours.

Peggy panicked. "A couple of hours? There's something wrong, Joel. The doctor specifically said five to six hours. So, what could've happened that it's taking longer than normal?"

"Peggy, we were just told the surgery is going well. That's good. Let's dwell on what we know and try not to guess about things we don't know."

At ten minutes past three, the doctor walked into the surgical waiting room. He said, "I'm sorry . . ."

Peggy collapsed into Joel's arms. The doctor appeared stunned. "Sit her down. Has she eaten today?"

Joel nodded. "We both had a big breakfast. She didn't want lunch. She fainted when you said you were sorry. Joey was her life."

"I'm confused. I was about to apologize for the surgery taking so much longer than I had told you, but it's not always easy to estimate these things. However, we were able to do everything we needed to do, and I feel good about the outcome."

A nurse was bathing Peggy's face. Joel knelt in front of her. "He's okay, Peg. Our baby is okay. He came through the surgery fine."

"But the doctor said—"

The doctor said, "Mrs. Jinright, you only heard a partial of my conversation and apparently misunderstood. I was apologizing for taking much longer than I had told you to expect. I realize how difficult it is to wait, especially when it's a child. But we had someone on our surgical team who had to be replaced at the last minute, through no fault of anyone's. The problem was handled as promptly as possible, and Joey's life was never in jeopardy due to the unexpected changes."

Joel hugged Peggy, and though she stiffened, she didn't pull away. She said, "Thank you, doctor. How long before I can take him home?"

"We'll keep him in ICU three or four days. It's standard procedure. Then we'll move him to a room where he'll remain for another several days."

Peggy said, "Can we see him now?"

"Not yet. Why don't you and your husband go down to the cafeteria and get something to eat? He tells me you didn't have lunch."

"I'm not hungry."

"You don't have to be hungry to eat a slice of their coconut cream pie. It'll remind you of your grandma's."

It was the first time she'd been able to smile since learning Joey would be having heart surgery. "How did you know my grandmother made the best coconut cream pie?"

He winked. "Didn't everyone's grandma?"

Joel said, "It does sound good. Why don't we try it, Peg?"

The doctor said, "Great. It'll be good for you both to get out of this room."

The pie was exactly as the doctor described. If Peggy had not known better she would have sworn someone had sneaked her grandmother's recipe. Neither of them had much to say. Finally, Peggy said what was really on her heart. "Joel, when the doctor referred to me as your wife, why didn't you correct him?"

He shrugged. "Why didn't you?"

"I felt it was your place."

His lip curled. "Why? Because it's the husband's place?"

"No. But it would've sounded better coming from you."

"Peggy, to tell the truth I had more pressing things on my mind and chatting with the doctor about our marital status was not a priority. Frankly, I don't care if he knows we're not married, and that Joey is *our* baby. If you'd like to explain your personal life with him, be my guest."

"You're angry."

"I'm not angry."

"Are you ready to go back upstairs?"

Joel nodded.

As they exited the elevator, they heard wailing down the hall. It appeared a young man was attempting to comfort his wife. A doctor with his head lowered was walking away.

Joel said, "Isn't that the couple you were talking to earlier?"

"Oh, my. It is. Greg and Laura. Their little girl was born prematurely three weeks ago."

"Looks as if they've just been given some bad news."

"Joel . . . what if we should lose Joey."

His heart raced. Not so much at the thought of losing Joey, because he dared not even go there—but did she say what if *we* should lose Joey?

Until now, she acted as if she produced a child all by herself. He mulled over his answer before responding. "We aren't going to lose him, Peg. But if we did, we'd bear one another's burden. We'd mourn together and lean on the Lord to be our comfort."

She nodded. "True. We need to pray for Greg and Laura. I can't imagine the hole that would be left in our hearts, if anything should happen to our sweet little Joey."

Was it his imagination, or was she trying to tell him that she was ready to acknowledge Joey had two parents?

CHAPTER 36

December 17th

Friday night, Deuce sat on the dock at Boggy Bayou, the way he often did at sundown. Seeing the sun set on the water could always calm him and bring a sense of peace after a stressful day. But lately, he'd been too happy to allow anything to cause stress. Even after being notified by SGT Restaurants, Inc. that the load of fish they ordered were spoiled and they were refusing to pay, Deuce didn't question it, even though he knew they were conning him.

So what? He'd write them off and chalk it up to lesson learned. It wasn't as if they were his biggest account. He stared at the brilliant colors reflecting like a giant kaleidoscope off the still waters, and marveled that he had such a peace. It was a new feeling. For months, he had tried to convince himself that he loved Maddie, and she loved him. Mr. Lopez had said, 'First love is different. It's special. It doesn't mean you can't love again. It can be just as special, but in a different way.' Maddie's letter had not broken his heart—it broke his pride. He was angry that she'd dare dump him. But once he dusted off his pride, he stood up to the fact that she only did what he should've done earlier.

Then Candy McCoy came into his life. He blinked to keep the wetness in his eyes from escaping. She loved him and he loved her. Together they could conquer anything.

Saturday morning, he arose early and dressed for his Mother's Christmas Dinner. He hated wearing suits and ties, but knowing how much it meant to his mom, he could do this for her. He'd try to make up for disappointing her on Thanksgiving.

He drove over to Candy's cottage, and before he could get out and walk to the door, she came running toward the truck. She looked beautiful, but he'd never seen her any other way. She had her hair all twisted up in what she called a French Twist and was wearing a black taffeta party dress with tiny spaghetti straps. In her hands was a fox stole. She looked like she was going to the Academy Awards, rather than to his Mom's Christmas Dinner.

Sliding over next to him, she pecked him on his lips. "Good Morning, my love." Pulling a tissue from her purse, she dabbed at the lipstick on his face.

He longed for the day he could wake up next to her and hear her repeat those beautiful words. He'd never tire of hearing her sweet voice.

She said, "I'm so nervous."

"Why would you be nervous?"

"What if your folks don't like me?"

"They will. I promise. And you'll love them."

Deuce had made the trip many times before, but today it seemed so much shorter. When they arrived, his dad was on the veranda and came out to the car. He hugged his son, and said, "This must be the beautiful Candy, you've told us about. Welcome!"

Ronald introduced himself, then hugged her as if she were a daughter. It brought tears to Candy's eyes. She'd always wondered what it would feel like to have a daddy. For the first time in her life, she felt she came close to understanding.

They went in the house and when Ramona hear her son's voice, she ran out of the kitchen with her arms stretched high in the air. Her face lit up. "You look so handsome, all dressed up in your suit. Thank you, sweetheart. I know you did it for me."

He glanced at Candy and blushed. He mumbled, "Didn't I tell you, I'm my mother's baby boy?"

Ramona rolled her eyes. "Of course you are. And you always will be." She reached over and hugged Candy. "Candy, I'm Ramona, and we are so glad to have you joining us." She stepped back and eyed Candy from head to foot. "My goodness, Deuce, you said she was pretty, but I didn't know you meant gorgeous. She's a doll."

Candy's lip quivered. "Thank you, ma'am. That's quite a compliment coming from you. You're very beautiful and look so

226

young to have a grown son."

Ramona laughed and hugged her once more. "Deuce, I love this girl."

"Me, too, Mom. And I'm glad you approve, because I plan to bring her to all our Christmas Dinners from here on out."

He glanced at his mom, then to Candy, and back to his mom. Ramona's mouth fell open. "Son, are you saying what I think you're saying?"

Candy looked wide-eyed, as if she might be wondering the same thing.

"I'm telling you what my plans are, Mom. I've yet to ask if this fits in with Candy's plans, but I'm ready to find out." He dropped to his knees in front of Candy and took her hand in his.

She whispered, "What are you doing?"

"I'm asking if you'll marry me, and come to all of Mom's Christmas Dinners, from here on out. You heard Mom. We love you."

She giggled. "I suppose if marrying you is the only way I can get an invitation, then the answer is a resounding, yes. Of course, I'll marry you. I thought you'd never ask."

Ronald was standing in the doorway. "I didn't realize you two had known each other that long."

Deuce laughed. "Dad, how long does it take? When you know, you know."

"Well, I can vouch for that. We'll be pleased to have you in the family, Candy."

Ramona said, "Excuse me, there's someone at the door. Could you get it, Ronald?"

Ronald came walking back to the parlor with Maddie Anderson by his side. Maddie spotted Deuce and squealed. "Deuce! Wow, look at you all spruced up. You look like you're ready for a wedding."

"Then Dad told you?"

"Told me what?"

He turned around and motioned for Candy. "Maddie, meet Candy, the girl I plan to marry."

"What?" The stunned look on her face was quickly replaced with laugher. "You dog. I thought you were serious for a minute there." She reached her hand out to Candy. "I'm Maddie. If you're a friend of the family, you've probably heard of me. Deuce and I were engaged."

"Nice to meet you Maddie, and yes, I have heard of you."

"Deuce is such a tease, but that's one of the reasons I love him. Now, tell me who you really are."

"I'm Candy—the girl Deuce plans to marry."

Total silence. Time seemed to stand still. Then Deuce said, "We're glad you were able to join us, Maddie. I haven't had time to tell everyone about your good news. Maddie was interviewed for head coach for the women's basketball team at Auburn University."

Ronald said, "Congratulations, Maddie. That's wonderful. I didn't even realize Auburn had a women's team. Well, I must say,

228

it's about time."

"Thank you, Mr. Jones, but Deuce hasn't heard the rest of the story. I was turned down."

Deuce felt as if the blood had drained from his face. "Oh, I'm so sorry. I was so sure—"

"Obviously, I was too, or I would never have made the decision I made—" She shrugged. "I don't suppose it matters now. Seems you've moved on. I don't mean to be a wet blanket. I'm happy for you, if this is really what you want, Deuce."

In order to shift the conversation topic, Ramona said "We'll eat as soon as Peggy and Joel get here. Peggy's little boy had surgery recently. She said they wouldn't be able to stay long, but they're planning to be here by twelve. Is everyone getting hungry?"

No one answered, and Ramona decided the tension in the room was even thicker than she'd previously suspected. She tried to think of something light to talk about, but her mind was blank. She cut her eyes over toward her son, who was standing near the kitchen door. She saw him whisper something to Candy.

With his head he made a light motion toward the front door. "Maddie, could I speak with you on the veranda?"

Her eyes darkened. "I'm not sure we have anything to say, Deuce."

"Maybe you don't, but I do. Please?"

Ramona, glanced over at Candy, who was wringing her hands. "Candy how are you at grating cabbage? I meant to make a bowl of slaw, and it slipped my mind. If we hurry, maybe we can get it done before Peggy and Joel arrive."

Candy's face lit up. "I'm a whiz at making slaw. Lead me to your grater."

Maddie walked out on the porch and plopped down in the swing. Deuce leaned against a column. She said, "Is she so jealous of me that you can't even sit beside me?"

"Maddie, stop it. You aren't going to make me feel any worse than I already feel. I'm sorry. I had no idea Mom had invited you until after I had asked Candy to come. I could tell you were embarrassed when I introduced you. I'm sure she was, too, and it was my fault. I realized afterward that I had handled the introductions poorly and I apologize."

She lowered her head. "No, Deuce, you pulled it off exactly the way it needed to go down, for all our sakes. I was about to make a fool of myself."

"I don't think that's possible."

"Oh, but it is. I came here with my pride shot to pieces. I was so sure I'd get the job that I gave up the best thing that had ever come my way. I suppose you know I'm talking about you. But seeing how quickly you found someone to replace me, I realize that you never really loved me, or it would've been impossible for you to toss me aside so quickly."

"Stop, Maddie. Think about what you're saying. Who tossed who aside? You were given a choice: Me, or a job. You chose the job."

"I was wrong, Deuce."

"I suppose you want me to say I was wrong, too . . . that I shouldn't have fallen in love so quickly."

"I see you're a mind-reader."

"No, but I probably know you better than you realize. You made a choice, and your number one choice didn't pan out, so you went down the line, and decided to settle for your second choice."

"That isn't true."

"You're in denial, Maddie. That's exactly what happened. But you saved us both."

"Saved us from what?"

"From making a big mistake. We were good together—as friends. We enjoyed one another's company, and we shared some good times together. Like the time we went to the Creek after church, and I talked you into hanging onto the vine with me. We pretended to be Tarzan and Jane, and we went swinging over the creek and—"

Her mouth gaped open. "Oh m'goodness, I've never been so scared as I was when that vine broke just as we swung over the creek."

"And you had on a new white dress."

"Yes, and the creek was overflowing since it had rained hard recently. The water was muddy, and you told me there were alligators in there."

"It was the truth. I've fished in that creek, and I've seen a couple of alligators. The vine never broke with Tarzan and Jane. I tried to act brave, but honestly, I was as terrified as you were."

When they stopped laughing, she said, "We really have had some good times, haven't we?"

"For sure. And I hope we'll always be friends."

"Me too. And I'm sorry I acted like such a heel. I've just discovered that a person will say some really stupid things when their pride is hurt." She giggled. "You really pulled a fast one, bud. By the way, she's very pretty, Deuce. I hope you'll both be very happy, and I sincerely mean that."

CHAPTER 37

Maddie and Deuce walked back into the house, and into the kitchen, headed straight toward Candy. She said, "Congratulations. I know I acted like a spoiled kid, but you must understand that I came with a speech ready, and Congratulations wasn't in my prepared salutatory address."

Candy felt a blush rising until she heard Maddie giggle. She felt the tension leaving her shoulders.

Maddie said, "It was really good. I had practiced it all the way from Troy, but once I saw you, I realized you were the one to give the address and I can't wait to hear it."

Still unsure how to take what Maddie was saying, Candy feigned a smile and thanked her. "Maddie, I'm sorry you were hurt. I know what it feels like, and I don't wish it on anyone."

"I know you don't. It's true I cared a lot for Deuce, but I think we both finally realized that if we had been in love, I wouldn't have chosen coaching over marrying him and he wouldn't have realized how much he loved you if he hadn't compared what you two have, with what we had. His love for you is for real." Then making light of the situation, she said, "However, I'm a little offended that I spent time worrying about him grieving over my letter, when in truth I was the farthest thing from his mind."

Candy laughed. "I'm sure that's not true." She handed her a fork. "Taste the slaw and see if you think we need to add more vinegar. It seems a little bland to me."

Maddie tried it, then smacked her lips. "Perfect." Then opening a cabinet door, she said, "I wonder if Ramona has any celery seed."

"Ooh, yes. That's exactly what it needs." Candy helped her shove jars around, then reached behind the cumin and pulled out a jar of celery seeds. Hearing loud voices coming from the parlor, they both stopped to listen. Candy said, "It sounds like we have more guests."

"Probably Peggy Jinright and her boss, Joel Gunter. They came to the Christmas dinner last year, and I remember Ramona saying she invited them again this year. Come on, and I'll introduce you."

As soon as they walked in Maddie heard a sweet little familiar voice, "Hey Aunt Maddie."

"Tina! Honey, what are you doing here? How did you get here?"

Then someone stepped out from behind the Christmas tree. "Hi, Sis."

She squealed. "Beau, what are you doing out?"

He laughed. "I didn't escape, if that's what you're thinking."

"What's going on? And how did you find me." Then throwing her hands in the air, she said, "I'm sorry folks. I forgot my manners. This is my brother, Beau, and he's been—uh he's been out of pocket and—"

"She's only half right. I am her brother Beau, but I haven't been out of pocket. I've been in prison, but I've been set free."

Ronald shook his hand. "That's great, Beau. I recall seeing news of the trial on TV. Can you share with us what happened?"

He said, "It's a long story, but I'm happy to tell it. Some of you may know that late last year, I was convicted of killing my wife. They said I was driving drunk and crashed into a tree, killing Trish. A witness testified that he came up on the wreck and there were only two of us in the car. He claimed I was the driver and Trish was the passenger. Three witnesses on three separate vehicles testified to seeing my car swerve all over the road, minutes before the fatal crash. The police officer wrote on the report that an open container of alcohol was found in the car. The report also said I was unable to walk a straight line." He glanced around at the stunned expressions. "From the looks in this room, I gather if you'd been on that jury, you would've sided with them."

Maddie said, "I love you, Beau. I'm glad you came."

"You love me, but you didn't trust me."

"You'll have to admit the evidence against you didn't look good. Are you saying you're really free? You don't have to go back to Prison?"

"I'm really free, sis."

"That's wonderful. I want to hear the whole story."

"The night it happened Trish didn't come home from work. I picked up Tina at the babysitters, went home and fixed our supper. That wasn't the first time my wife failed to come home. I knew she was seeing someone. When she still wasn't home at nine o'clock, I decided to go looking for her. I called the sitter and told her we had an emergency to come up and could she keep Tina overnight? She told me to bring her over."

Maddie said, "Was Trish with a man when you found her?"

"Hold on. I'm getting to it. I rode around for hours, going to every honky-tonk within fifty miles, looking for her car. I'd almost given up when I rounded the corner on County Road 4, and I saw a car that looked like it was trying to climb a tree. Then I realized it was Trish's car. I pulled off the road and ran down the ravine. She was alone, although she was pinned in on the passenger's side. I figured she was thrown over there from the impact. My emotions were going haywire. I was torturing myself for thinking the worst of her. I concluded she was probably on her way home from work when an animal ran out in front of her, causing her to lose control. The door on the passenger side was bashed in, so I crawled in on the driver's side to see if she was still alive. Blood was everywhere. The next thing I knew, I came to, and—"

Deuce said, "Hold on. I think I missed something. You came to? Are you saying you fainted?"

"No. I was knocked out."

Maddie said, "But you said there was no one there."

"I said Trish was the only one in the car. I had assumed she was alone. As I was saying, I came to, heard loud sirens, and saw flashing bright lights. Two policemen were dragging me out of the car and demanding that I walk. I was dizzy. My head hurt and I reeked of alcohol. I vaguely remember being pushed into a squad car, and I woke up later in jail."

Deuce said, "I can understand why a jury might've found you guilty. I would've had a lot of questions too, if I'd been on the jury. I'm still having trouble understanding how you could've been freed, after a jury found you guilty."

Ramona frowned. "Deuce! He's been tried once. He doesn't need us to try him again. I'm sure there's more to his story."

Beau said, "It's okay ma'am. I agree with him. It sounds mighty suspicious."

Maddie said, "Beau, you're telling the truth, aren't you? You didn't escape?"

"No, sis. I won't deny I thought about it a few times, knowing I was in there for ten years, and Tina would be all grown up by the time I got out."

"So, how *did* you get out?"

"You've heard it said, 'there's no fury like a woman scorned?' Well, that's what happened. Doug Pearson was our realtor when we bought our house, and he's the one Trish had been sneaking out with, though I didn't know it at the time.

His wife had caught them together once before, but he promised her it was over. Then, when she heard about the accident on TV, she called her husband at work to tell him, but he yelled at her and told her not to talk about the accident with anyone. He told her I had already been arrested and if she mentioned anything about his previous affair with Trish, the police might want to question him, and it could hurt his business.

She said Doug had become an alcoholic, and she noticed that every time something about my trial would come on TV, he'd change channels. It wasn't until she ran the vacuum under the bed, and it sucked up a corner of a bloody shirt that she put two and two together. When she showed it to him, he grabbed it from her hands, put his hands to her throat, and threatened to choke her if she mentioned that shirt to anyone. He built a fire in the fireplace and threw it into the fire, then drank himself into a stupor.

After that, he became more abusive than in the past. She said she wanted to go to the police, but she was afraid of him. She said she couldn't bear to think of my little girl growing up without a mother or a daddy, while I served time in prison for something I didn't do. The guilt became overwhelming.

So, the other night, when he was drunk, she turned on the tape recorder and got him to admit that he was the one driving the car. She said he seemed gleeful as he told how it all went down. He said whenever I leaned over trying to see if Trish was alive, he hit

238

me over the head, knocking me out. Then he poured a can of beer on me and hid in the bushes. She said he laughed as he recounted his actions, saying he ran across the road, got into my car, and drove it back to my house, then walked home. They only lived two blocks away. He sneaked in his house at three-thirty and stuffed the bloody clothes under the bed. His wife was asleep in another bedroom."

Beau blew out a lungful of air. "She got it all on tape and took it to the police. But she had more. Before she showed him the shirt, she snipped off part of the cuff that was blood soaked, since she had predicted he would take the shirt from her when she confronted him with it.

So, she not only had his taped confession, she had Trish's blood on a portion of his shirt. The same shirt he was wearing in a picture taken that day of him with a client who had just closed on one of his properties.

I had no idea any of this was taking place until my lawyer showed up last night, telling me I was a free man. I picked up Tina early this morning and the housemother told me you had left this address in case they might need to get in touch with you."

Maddie threw her arms around her big brother. "I'm so happy for you, I could cry."

He reached up and with his handkerchief brushed a tear from her face. "Could?" He laughed.

Ramona's eyes were glistening. "I don't think you're the only one fighting back the tears, Maddie. What a wonderful ending to such a tragic story."

CHAPTER 38

The doorbell rang but before anyone could answer the door, Peggy and Joel came walking inside. Joel yelled out, "Time to eat, the Gunters are here."

Ramona wiped her hands on her apron and hugged them both. Then, eyeing them suspiciously, she said, "Something funny is going on."

Joel said, "Funny? I don't sese anything funny, do you darling?"

Peggy said, "Nope. I can't imagine what's funny."

Ramona's jaw dropped. "Wait. Tell me again what you said when y'all walked in, Joel."

He looked at Peggy as if he needed help recalling his words. "Peg? Do you remember?"

She looked bewildered. "If I remember correctly, you said, "The Gunters' have arrived.' I don't remember anything after that."

Ramona laughed out loud. "Then, it's true?"

Ronald said, "I still don't get it."

Peggy held out her left hand, showing off a gold band.

His jaw dropped. "The Gunters! Now, I get it. Well, Congratulations and Merry Christmas to you both. I think that's wonderful." The others rushed over to congratulate the happy couple.

Ronald said, "Either I've been left out of the loop, or this happened rather suddenly."

Joel said, "Neither. There was no loop, but it wasn't sudden. It was way past due."

Ramona said, "I think I'm about to cry. I'm so happy for you both. Now tell us how little Joey is doing."

Joel and Peggy took turns sharing the events of the past week and a half. There had been ups and downs, but they both felt confident that little Joey was doing fine. Even better than expected. Peggy said "Joel and I have been under a dark cloud since learning Joey would be undergoing heart surgery. But that cloud had a silver lining. We were both too stubborn to admit how much we loved one another. I was afraid of rejection, since I'd gone through it with him once and couldn't bear to go through it again. And then I discovered he was afraid that I would reject him."

Joel put his arm around her waist. He said, "Who could've blamed her? I was a heel to ever let her go. I had to hit bottom before I could look up. And when I did, I knew there'd never be anyone else for me. But I had blown it. I convinced myself that she hated me. When she took the job at the office, I decided I was wrong. She didn't hate me. She didn't even think about me one way or the other. I was out of her mind, and she was out of my league. I was convinced it was over, and nothing I could do could reverse the damage I'd done."

Peggy said, "Frank was a good man. I loved him for being so good to me and Joey, and I'll always be grateful for all he did for us. But you were never out of my mind, Joel. I wanted to believe I hated you for the way you were destroying yourself. But if I had truly hated you, I wouldn't have cried so much, because I wouldn't have cared so much. I wouldn't have spent so many sleepless nights, thinking of what could've been."

It was time to sit down and eat, yet Maddie was still on the phone. Minutes later, she ran back in apologizing for holding up dinner. "But I have some great news. That was Coach Weeks. She said the girl who was given the Coaching position wants me as her assistant. I'm so excited. She's terrific and I know we'll work well together. She deserved the position. She's had experience coaching on a full court. I'll learn a lot from her."

All the food was on the table, except the meat. Ramona had given Candy the privilege of bringing it in from the kitchen, and everyone oohed and ahhed over a beautiful baked ham, gaily decorated with pineapple slices and maraschino cherries.

Ramona announced that it was a Jones tradition to go around the table telling something you were thankful for on Thanksgiving.

"Since we didn't have the traditional Thanksgiving Dinner this year, I'd like to use this time to voice our thanks. I'll go first." Ramona said she was thankful to have a working oven so she could cook a holiday meal and have wonderful friends to join with them to share the bounty.

She invited everyone to tell something for which they were thankful. No one seemed to have trouble coming up with a ready answer. Deuce and Candy were thankful that they would soon become one; Maddie was thankful for the opportunity to become an Assistant Coach at Auburn. But then she added, "I'm also thankful for Deuce—my very special friend. I've had a lot of disappointments in my lifetime, and unfortunately, I quickly learned that if I couldn't have what I wanted, to settle for second best."

Deuce rolled his eyes and grinned. "Second best—that would be me, folks."

Maddie laughed. "You're the one who labeled yourself as second best. But you helped me realize I was wrong to give up on my dream, and that's exactly what I was willing to do. It's what I've always done. So, I thought if I couldn't coach, I'd marry. But Deuce helped me to see what a dreadful mistake that would've been for us both. I needed to stay focused on my goal and not give up on something I truly wanted."

Beau was next. He said, "I think I've already had my turn. But I do want to thank the Good Lord for the miracle for which I prayed. To be honest, I felt I was asking for the impossible, yet I kept praying, hanging on to that scripture that says, 'There's nothing impossible with God.'"

Tina said, "My turn?"

Beau nodded. "Sure, baby. What are you thankful for today?"

She looked up into her daddy's eyes. "You. I wanted you to come home, so I prayed, too."

When it came Joel's time to share, he shed tears as he tried to get the words out. Peggy put her hand on his shoulder and finished for him.

"Joel and I are so thankful for our sweet little baby and the fact that he came through the surgery. He's such a blessing."

Joel leaned over and kissed her. He said, "And we're also thankful that we didn't allow foolish pride to prevent us from being a family. It took swallowing a lot of Humble Pie, before we got the strength to admit being right wasn't nearly as important as being together."

Ronald said, "Wow. What a day this has been already. If it gets any better, I don't know if I can stand it. Ramona and I are so very thankful to have had all of you sitting around our table today, sharing your good news.

Please bow your heads, and let's Thank God for whom all blessings flow."

****

The Vietnam war escalated in the years to come. Babies were born and people died. The Beatles were the rage, Nixon became President, Elvis films became popular, Beehives were in style, but the really great event in the 1960's took place in the Boondocks on Boggy Bayou in Jinx Bay, Florida. The townsfolk had united and to this day, Christmas in the Boondocks continues to draw huge crowds from far and near.

KAY CHANDLER BOOKS

JINX BAY SERIES

Cannery Road – Book 1
Boggy Bayou – Book 2
Christmas in the Boondocks -Book 3

VINEGAR BEND SERIES

Chalkboard Preacher from Vinegar Bend – Book 1
Drawing Conclusions -Book 2
A Clean Slate – Book 3
2 x 2 - Book 4
No Crib for a Bed- Book 5
While Mortals Sleep- Book 6

SWITCHED SERIES

Lunacy – Book 1
Unwed – Book 2
Mercy – Book 3

GRAVE ENCOUNTER SERIES

When the Tide Ebbs – Book 1
When the Tide Rushes In – Book 2
When the Tide Turns – Book 3

THE KEEPER SERIES

The Keeper – Book 1
The Prey – Book 2
The Destined – Book 3

HOMECOMING SERIES

Sweet Lavender –-Book 1
Unforgettable – Novella - 2
Gonna Sit Right Down – Novella- 3
Hello Walls – Novella - 4

PLOW HAND –-Stand-alone
A GIRL CALLED ALABAMA –- Stand-alone
SWAMP ANGEL-Stand-alone

Made in the USA
Columbia, SC
21 December 2024

50200925R00150